In His Head

Ron Sobolewski

Printed in the United States of America
Library of Congress Control Number: 2019917765
ISBN: Softcover 978-1-64376-557-00
eBook 978-1-64376-556-3

Republished by: PageTurner, Press and Media LLC
Publication Date: November 14, 2019

To order copies of this book, contact:
PageTurner, Press and Media
Phone: 1-888-447-9651
order@pageturner.us
www.pageturner.us

In His Head

Contents

Before I begin, I wish to express a deep appreciation for the 1960 World Champion Pittsburgh Pirates. They provided a little boy with an enduring love and passion for the beautiful game of baseball. The following is the list and sequence of those players as they are listed in this narrative.

(A) Vernon Law, (B) Gene Baker, (C) Smoky Burgess, (D) Rocky Nelson, (E) Harvey Haddix, (F) Bob Skinner, (G) Hal Smith, (H) Dick Stuart, (I) Fred Green, (J) Danny Kravitz, (K) Don Hoak, (L) Dick Schofield, (M) Tom Cheney, (N) Clem Labine, (O) Vinegar Ben Mizell, (P) Joe Gibbon, (Q) Bill Virdon, (R) Dick Groat, (S) Roy Face, (T) Bob Friend, (U) Joe Christopher, (V) Roberto Clemente, (W) Bob Oldis, (X) Bill Mazeroski, and (Y) Gino Cimoli.

None of the characters portrayed in this effort are real. All of the events depicted in this book were invented. None ever took place. This is nothing more than my attempt to entertain.

"Colerain Pike, the Genuine True Man"

A true man was one "who does not make the poor man conscious of his poverty, an obscure man his obscurity, or any man of his inferiority or deformity; who is himself humbled if necessity compels him to humble another; who does not flatter wealth, cringe before power, or boast of his own possessions or achievements; who speaks with frankness but always with sincerity and sympathy; whose deed follows his word."

—(John Walker Wayland, 1899)

Chapter 1

"MAN IS THE ONLY CREATURE WHO CAN KILL TO KILL"

His blue jeans, stonewashed and faded, formerly belonged to a man of considerable size. They were cracked and wrinkled in the knees, bore a degree of soiling, twice rolled up at the waist, and held in place by an unevenly woven leather belt. The jeans were manufactured to fit a size 38-inch waist and a 34-inch inseam. Comically, too large for their wearer, they were also double-cuffed to prevent him from tripping. He wore smudged and stained white canvass Nike brand hi-top basketball sneakers. His obviously oversized navy blue pea coat, with one of the large front buttons missing, complemented his shopping ensemble. On his face, faux eyeglasses gave the contact lens-wearing shopper his desired bug-eyed, insect appearance. Compulsively, he scratched at his head through his black woolen ski cap. Actually, he kept his carefully cut hair an inch in length on the crest of his head, with the remaining hair on the sides and back closely cropped at one-eighth of an inch.

His targeted store was located in the all-black, middle-class neighborhood known as Springtown. The small brass bells wired to the entrance's double glass doors clinked and shivered as he thrust open the "in" door on his right. He intentionally allowed in a sudden rush of early winter wind that seemed to propel him into the "Red, Black, and Green" thrift store. He scanned, located, and then painfully ambled over to the shoe department located in the rear of the spacious facility. Intentionally he hunched over, indicating that he might be burdened by a possible hunchback deformity. He tried not to appear too kyphotic. Each of the employees and all of the other shoppers were Americans of African descent. His whiteness easily stood out among them. He perceived himself as an isolated desert atoll situated amongst a chain of lush, vegetated islands.

The shopper began to examine pairs of gently worn work boots. He handled and then carelessly dropped several pairs before selecting a pair of black 8-inch-high "Quarry" brand boots. They displayed a tractor wheel pattern of excellent remaining tread, unbroken shoelaces, with all of the aglets securely in place. The fact that they were size 11 1/2 and that he wore a size 10 did not matter to him. His primary consideration was to purchase a pair of boots with an excellent tread depth with a detectable pattern. As a boot was slipped over each of his hands, he noted the $6.00 price tag. "Perfect," he thought.

The cashier that he selected to approach was about twenty years old, tall, lean, and facially attractive. Her tightly braided hair segments were gathered and pulled back into a ponytail descending along her neck and then spraying onto her shoulder tops. As the shopper entered her cash register lane, he spied her name tag: Vernonella Law. [A]

He blurted out, "How you say your name?"

Politely, she responded phonetically, "Ver-non-ella."

"I'm buyin' these boots for six dollars," he announced.

"Well, Mister, this is your lucky day, because today, our store has a special sale—10 percent off on all purchases," she responded.

"I don't have ten dollars—only six," he implored.

"No, no, no, wait," she interrupted. "What is your name?" she asked.

Seemingly stunned, he replied cautiously, "Alfred."

"Listen, Alfred," she explained, "these boots will cost less than six dollars because you get a discount today."

He stared at her with an expression of puzzled bewilderment.

"Alfred, your bill is $5.40 with the 10 percent discount," she said as she read the cash register sales receipt.

"How you figure that discount?" he inquired.

"Well, you divide $6.00 by 10, then you subtract that number—60 cents—from $6.00 and you get $5.40," she explained.

"I get the boots and change," he agreed.

Vernonella slipped the boots and the receipt into a green plastic bag and handed the package to her beaming customer. He took hold of the bag with his left hand and with his right, accepted two quarters and a dime in change from his $5.40 purchase.

"Bye-bye, Ver-non-ella," he said.

"'Bye, Alfred," she responded.

At the next register, another cashier, Eugena Baker [B], commented. "That was some simple, old white fool, Wasn't it?"

Vernonella Law replied softly, "Aw, just let him alone."

The advertised color of his 2006 Ford Ranger pick-up truck was cinnamon apple red. The truck was parked at the far edge of the strip mall parking lot, denying its view to anyone in the thrift store. He climbed into the unlocked cab, locked the door, and removed the black boots from their plastic carrying bag. On the passenger seat rested a 100-unit bag of pure white cotton balls. He began inserting the cottony forms into the toes of his newly purchased boots. He needed to insure that those size 11 1/2 boots fit comfortably onto his size 10 feet.

As an integral facet of his evolving and meticulous planning, he deliberately needed to be noticed. Identifiable as an odd, older white man buying a pair of used boots at an all-black business. Yes, the shopper needed to be identified, but only as his crafted ruse was to be presented.

Chapter 2

"KILLING NEED NOT BE COMMITTED WITH RAGE"

While deliberately driving away from Springtown, he removed his baggy jeans by deftly sliding them down over his black colored "And Now" brand wind pants, size 34x30 inches. He turned right onto Hankbert Boulevard and began driving in the direction of his northern suburban home. He slowed his truck, made a right turn, and slipped into the parking lot of a Food Nation grocery market. Behind the expansive and flat commercial building were three large battleship gray-colored dumpsters. He tossed the jeans, pea coat, ski cap, and sports shoes into the middle receptacle, simply because it had its gaping lid opened. He surveyed and examined the well-drawn and artistically spray-painted name "ZAYFO" tagged upon the outer side of bin number three. The green and white letters on a black background presented an admirable design and optimal use of the available space.

"Damn good design," he muttered to himself. "I wonder why so many citizens automatically criticize the young artists who carefully, and with obvious skill, create some great designs." He continued, "I guess those valuable urban canvasses of bridge pillars, abandoned buildings, and forgotten concrete walls should be untouchable.

"Civic organizations should welcome and offer opportunities and possibly seek seed money for programs and places for tagger artists to practice their skills."

Basking with inner satisfaction, he had obtained his boots, knowing that he would be able to leave them as information after the completion of the first segment of his impending series of tasks. He was compelled to submit to a period of rest to formulate, plan, and review for his impending life-altering actions.

Chapter 3

"KILLING HAS NOTHING TO DO WITH GOD"

The United States Selective Service System conducted its 1971 annual lottery draft on July 1 for young men turning eighteen years old, born in 1953. Three hundred and sixty-six individual slips of paper, each containing a date of the year, were placed into separate plastic capsules. They were hand-mixed in a shoe box and then dumped into a deep, glass jar. The capsules were drawn, one at a time, from the jar and recorded. It was projected that the draft call would go out to individuals born on the first 125 dates selected.

Colerain would be turning eighteen on July 29. His birth date was the fourth date drawn (004). He had previously decided not to attend college for a year or so after his high-school graduation. He had graduated with honors with a significant number of his classes listed on the "honors" level. Colerain had been accepted at several prestigious universities, including Dartmouth and the University of Pennsylvania. He wanted to delay admission for one year to travel and gain some real-life work experience. Sufficient funds for college were never to be an issue. His father, Borland, was an abundantly successful investment banker, and his mother, Tenley, was a pediatrician in a thriving practice. Colerain was their only child, and he lived in a comfortable and loving family environment.

He had heard and read about the war in Southeast Asia. He studied in detail the battle at Dien Bin Phu and the French defeat there. He knew of the Tet Offensive, Khe Shan, and the battle for the ancient city of Hue. He knew that General Vo Nguyen Giap was the supreme commander of the Vietnam People's Army, the regional Viet Cong, and that they were unrelenting adversaries. Facing induction, assuming that he would be pronounced 1-A, he resigned himself to the probability that he would be joining the United States Army.

Within three weeks a postcard arrived at his home announcing the date, time, and location for his determining physical examination. In high school Colerain was a three-sport athlete. During the fall season he ran cross-country. He medaled at the state championships, coming in fourth place out of forty-eight select runners. He participated in the winter sports season by joining the school swimming team. He swam the breaststroke and competed in long-distance events, the 800- and 1,600-yard challenges. He displayed endurance and a capacity to swim long distances at a steady and regulated rate. During the spring sports season he excelled at baseball as a fleet-footed center fielder and as a reliable relief pitcher with a fastball thrown consistently in the high eighties.

The pre-induction physical was rudimentary. A basic heart and lung examination with a stethoscope was quickly performed. Height, weight, and a blood pressure reading were taken. A one-minute eye exam, which identified Colerain's vision at 15/20, a hearing test, plus a quick dental exam and teeth count. Finally, a urine sample was required before Colerain was free to exit the testing center. Within one week Colerain Pike received his fitness rating from the armed services. He was listed as 1-A. Fit for active duty in the armed forces without restriction.

Chapter 4

"LIFE WILL PRESENT UNCHARTED CHALLENGES"

On Friday, August 20, 1971, Colerain signed for a registered letter, addressed to him, delivered by the U.S. Postal Service from United States Department of the Army. Contents of the mailing included his date of induction for basic training, the location (Fort Knox, Kentucky), a list of necessary personal items, and two Greyhound bus tickets. The first ticket would take him to Louisville and the second to Radcliff, Kentucky, near the Fort Knox military reservation.

Eleven days later Colerain was riding on a Greyhound "Scenic Cruiser," seated mid-bus on the driver's side (reportedly among the safest seats on large commercial vehicles). He enjoyed his last week of civilian life with friends. He dined out, drove around visiting favorite and familiar locales with friends, slept in until mid-morning, and went to the movies. (He saw *Klute* and *Billy Jack*, among others.) Colerain's parents, previously expressing strong anti-war sentiments, were less than enthusiastic about their son's decision to go on active duty. They proposed college and its deferment, an army reserve unit, or an easily orchestrated health condition. Colerain remained steadfast in his decision to allow his true fate to be unveiled. He would serve, as required, in the United States Army.

Chapter 5

"THE PAST IS NEVER DEAD, IT'S NOT EVEN PAST" (W. FAULKNER)

The day after Thanksgiving, the last Friday of the month, would provide a welcome opportunity for a single and unattached woman to remain alone in her home, condo, or apartment to regain her essential solitude. She had just visited with family and indulged her aging parents. She openly bonded with siblings, nephews, and nieces; yet, she eagerly anticipated returning to her private and singular residence. She is relaxed living alone, preferring her space and her delicate possessions. This independent woman settles into her complete freedom knowing that she can use family, friends and co-workers any time that contacts and interactions are needed. Her preference is to be alone. That has become her comfortable and required lifestyle.

Travel, a new vehicle, the latest fashion, and dining out are easily obtainable. The professional, well-educated and independent woman is to be respected and envied, isn't she?

So what if she complains occasionally about not being able to find a "good" man in her age bracket. So what if most of her male friends and co-workers that she feels comfortable with are gay. So what if she makes comments about the broad shoulders or tight ass of some dark-haired young man twenty-five years her junior.

So what if she indicates the newly hired salesman, at her place of employment, is hitting on her. So what, she is comfortably settled, and doesn't plan on doing anything to disrupt the sereneness she has earned.

On one isolated occasion, she almost visited an adult, exotic book/movie store named Zoticerotica. But she froze, maybe from an avalanche of guilt or embarrassment, which compelled her to slowly drive past the store's parking lot entrance. She surfed the Internet at home, often entering a voyeur site that offered women an opportunity to enjoy images of nude males in public settings. She surprised herself by relishing the photos offered by the website. Periodically, she had daydreams about a certain young man whom she had a six-month relationship with when she was twenty years old. He was bright, athletic, attractive, and besides, he pursued her with charming vigor. He claimed that she was the most expensive and most desired of candies, and he would not stop pursuing her until he had the pleasure of enjoying her. She savored that example of his wooing. On sultry summer evenings he met with her at their neighborhood's public park. Usually, he wore basketball shorts, flip-flops, and a white wife-beater T-shirt. She felt comfortable wearing hot pants or short shorts with a ribbed tube top. They could not keep their eyes from each other. She told him that he looked like Adonis and then indicated that she had a difficult time not touching or putting her lips all over him.

Unfortunately, her mother constantly indicated that she didn't like or trust this young man. When he came to visit at her family's apartment, the hostile mother baited him into arguments and disagreements about insignificant topics. If she could not bully the high school graduate, she became irritated and demanded that he leave, barely providing her daughter with an opportunity for proper good-byes.

He would call Erica and her mother would conveniently forget to tell her of time frames or fail to divulge stated plans or time together. Slowly, Erica began to distrust and lose patience with his emotional attempts to offer explanations that seemed to be a constant requirement because of her mother's interference.

When Erica asked "Why didn't you call?" questions, he responded passionately that he had called twice and spoke with her mother on both occasions. Often, she replied that her mother said, "Your boyfriend never phoned." And sometimes, in anger, she added that she did not trust Colerain as far as she could throw him.

Erica was eye-candy pretty, with silky and blemish-free facial features. Her long dark hair framed her face that exhibited seductive dark eyes with extended eyelashes. The cupid's bow of her upper lip was perfect in form, and he became pleasantly addicted to kissing her. Her long hair was often pulled back from her face in a ponytail style. That tail would move and bounce in tandem with her perky body movements. Her ethnic background was a blend of Lebanese Christian, Serbian and Northern Italian. Those identities meant little to her all-American friend, whose constant thoughts emphasized her brightness, beauty, and extreme desirableness.

On many occasions she offered her bared breasts to him for their mutual enjoyment, and he devoured those offerings. When she felt completely isolated, and guaranteed that no interruptions or unexpected visitors would embarrass them, she would provide Colerain with the delights of an oral experience. Erica knew that they were progressing very rapidly to actual sexual intercourse. She was prepared to offer Colerain her protected virginity at the earliest possible opportunity. They both became easily aroused in each other's presence and the time and circumstance for "going all the way" appeared to be inevitable. Colerain revealed to Erica that she was "in his head" and that he enjoyed his detailed images of her frequently.

The pressure from Erica's mother, and her comments, continued like the considerable year-round snowfall that falls upon the higher elevations of Colorado's Rocky Mountains. Some of Erica's friends criticized Colerain to her because of his cavalier behavior toward them in mixed company. These pressures and opinions began to wear upon her. Colerain became agitated at what he thought were baseless accusations and implications about his behavior. Sometimes, he verbally sparred with his accusers. Yet, somehow, he never responded with disrespectful anger to her mother. He found himself biting his tongue on numerous occasions. The constant negative reactions eventually proved to be erosive, and Erica succumbed to the pressure of maintaining her relationship with her mother. She decided that she wanted some time away from Colerain to reassess their relationship.

He was just plain pissed, yet he remained completely under control when he stated to her, "Just forget the whole thing." Separation appeared to be easy because his male ego and street credibility needed to be maintained. He was sure he could entertain any other of many young ladies who have indicated interest in him.

Currently, thirty-some years after their relationship ended, Erica remained in his head. He was virtually unable to eliminate his thoughts or images of her. Inadvertently, and from a distance, he had seen her on two or three occasions during the elapsing two and one half decades. During that time no words were ever spoken between them. No contact was ever attempted, yet still, the relentless visions of her had never receded. His focus was unwavering on this the Friday after the Thanksgiving holiday of 2011. He would pay her a most memorable final visit.

Chapter 6

"WITH EVERY CHOICE LIES THE POSSIBILITY OF REGRET"

Chapman-Hayes County provides property owners with an Internet website that permits any viewer access to all property transactions within its boundaries. The website offers owners, buyers, and sellers names, dates, values, locations, informational details, and photographic images of all private property owned, sold, or purchased throughout the county. It was quite simple and expeditious for him to gain access to all of the information he sought about Erica and her modest home. All that Colerain was required to do was to type in her maiden name and the regularly updated system provided the desired details in a matter of seconds.

Erica purchased her home on July 16, 1992, for $71,000 from Richard and Margaret Stuart. The Union Central Bank of Pennsylvania holds the property deed on her twenty-five-year mortgage note at a reasonable rate of 6¼ percent. The assessed value of her home in November 2007 was $90,000. Her property taxes were quite affordable.

The house consisted of six rooms, of which three are bedrooms, 1 1/2 baths, A/C, and natural gas heating. A posted photograph of the house reveals a one-car integral garage, a small slab front porch, and several dense evergreen bushes surrounding the structure. Playing to a hunch, he navigated to the informational page on the website and typed in the address next door to her house, 972 Calipso Street. Erica's home address is 970 Calipso. Amazing good luck, he thought, 972 Calipso has been up for sale at $88,000 since September 30, 2011. The home was being offered by agent Forrest Burgess [C] representing Evergreen Realty at a telephone number, 418-611-7800.

On the Wednesday prior to the holiday, Colerain decided to take an early evening drive-by to her home between 4:45 and 5:00 p.m. to determine when total darkness would probably occur. He estimated that it would be a pitch-black and moonless evening by no later than 5:15 p.m. He would scout a parking location for his pick-up and determine a sense of the street and private property lighting. Her home was provided with abundant cover from neighbor and street traffic. She should have trimmed back those evergreen bushes and shrubs years ago. Her immediate next-door neighbors seemed to prefer similar natural privacy providers. Crime statistics for the neighborhood were low and many homeowners tend to let their guards down intentionally when they feel safe and comfortable. There were no signs of Erica owning a pet who would be able to sound alarms. There is an immeasurable value to having a dog, any dog, because it is in their nature to protect by sounding vocal warnings. There was no fencing or tie-out runs to indicate that there was a dog on the premises

He knew not to make any traceable phone calls in any attempt to ascertain patterns when Erica would be at home. Of course, he could use a public pay phone that had no municipal cameras mounted nearby to determine her at-home time tendencies. She was listed in the Crossover telephone company directory under E. Stamcic, 970 Calipso, 418-611-2877. For a minimum of $2.75 per month, this single woman could have been slightly more secure and less traceable. For just $33 per year, she could have had an unlisted private phone number, probably the cost of getting her nails done at Victoria's Asian Nails where she visited regularly every three weeks.

He would use Evergreen Realty's Forrest Burgess as his ploy to validate his presence in Erica's neighborhood to gain her trust. He will be searching for a smaller home, in a safe neighborhood for his seventy-five-year-old mother. Her lifelong city community was becoming seedy with a growing number of Section Eight properties being offered there. Too often, with those housing arrangements, individuals and families have little or no interest in maintaining property values or contributing to the stability of the area. Then, crime seemed to flourish.

During his planned, scouting drive-by, he noticed an United Parcel Service package on Erica's front porch with a prominent label announcing that "Snow Angel Babies" were enclosed. He noted that she must be a collector of objects to some degree and he surmised that her pet-less home must be as neat as a pin. She probably didn't welcome too many visitors, and at fifty-two years of age, she was undoubtedly very set in her ways.

Chapter 7

"THE NINE-MINUTE VISIT"

A steady snowfall was blanketing every tangible object except for the occasional circular-shaped street sewer lid, which remained steam heated and dark and readable. Colerain parked his truck in mid-block, knowing that the snow would continue to fall and within minutes coat his vehicle with a snowy soft cover. No street light was shining on this section of Calipso Street and there was an assortment of shrubs to conceal him if he needed to be concealed.

He traversed about 150 feet, walking quickly, reaching 970 Calipso in seconds. He wore his cotton ball-filled size 11 1/2 black work boots, black Rogue brand slacks, a lambskin black leather jacket, and black leather gloves. A wheat-colored pullover, made of cashmere, completed his dressy ensemble.

He stepped carefully along the short sidewalk, then up three steps to the small concrete slab porch. Colerain attempted to wipe the snow from his boots on a rubber outdoor floor mat. He pushed the pineapple-shaped doorbell and two sharp buzzing bursts resulted. It was 5:17 p.m. and total darkness had descended. The porch light flicked on within in a second or two, and the wooden front door and the full-length glass storm door opened without a question or challenge. Why didn't this independent, single woman look, listen, and ask before providing possible access to an unexpected visitor? Maybe, just maybe, her neighborhood was really secure, or she may have had a general idea of who would be ringing her doorbell.

He immediately offered Erica information about his purported meeting with the Evergreen Realty agent Mr. Burgess, while not looking directly at Erica to avoid any possible instantaneous recognition. Within seconds of his introduction, Erica recognized him, his short hair notwithstanding.

With a pleasant smile and excited tone, she gushed. "Oh my, Colerain, Colerain Pike, come in here, and get out of that snowstorm."

He observed her naturally aging yet still very attractive face and feigning sudden recognition, he replied, "Oh my God, Erica Stamcic! Do you live here?"

"Yes, get in here," she announced in a voice brimming with apparent glee.

Without touching any part of her front door, he stepped into her open living room and gently pushed it closed with his gloved left hand, hoping that she did not notice. While she welcomed him in and offered him a seat, he wiped his boots on a woven floor mat and stepped toward her.

As Erica was turning around to face him, his right hand had already entered his right jacket pocket and he withdrew a stainless steel piano wire. The wire was 24 inches in length and made of tightly wound steel strands, producing a flexible 14 gauge steel wire with finger rings attached to its ends. In the military this wire was sometimes used in strangulation assaults against an enemy or rival. He spun Erica away from himself and quickly wrapped the wire around her wrinkle-free neck. His powerful hands, wrists, and forearms, made rock hard from years of working with weights, forced the wire tightly around her throat. Erica was explosively overcome with heart-pounding terror and shock. She was instantly sapped of any ability to breathe, struggle, or speak. She remained upright, thoroughly denied the smallest gasp of necessary aeration as Colerain made three more intensely powerful pulls upon the ever-tightening wire.

At that instant, Colerain quietly stated, "Erica, the time has arrived to remove you from my head."

Her eyes had rolled back into her head as her attractive countenance was frozen in horror, and her sleek neck was beginning to display some noticeable shades of purple as blood vessels were bursting internally. Colerain continued the viselike grip for a few more seconds as her body slumped and sagged against him. He lifted her 110-pound body and gently laid her upon the aqua-colored carpeting between her coffee table and her 46-inch flat screen television. The wire was returned to his right front jacket pocket.

He undressed Erica quickly, neatly folding then laying her sweater, sweat pants, white socks, 34C white bra, and hipster-style panties on a nearby sectional couch. He placed her arms alongside her body and slightly opened her legs to reveal a modest growth of dark pubic hair. Her breasts, by their own weight, fell laterally to her body's sides. He tenderly closed her eyes and moved her slightly gray streaked ponytail to the right side of her head.

Without removing his form-fitting leather gloves, he paused to look upon Erica. A fine-looking woman, he reflected. From his left front jacket pocket he removed a yellow Slick disposable razor, a black permanent marker, and five thin tipped highlighter markers. The colors of the markers were all light and bright: they were pink, lime green, yellow, light blue, and tangerine.

Using the Slick razor, he shaved some of the hair in Erica's pubic region, providing her with the bikini-cut styling. He removed the smallest stubble and brushed the hair segments onto the carpet between her legs. He then closed her legs for a more modest presentation.

Between her breasts, in the area around her sternum, he used the black permanent marker to draw the profile of a long-haired young man. He also worked in some color shading using the highlighter markers.

The drawing was about 8 inches high by 6 inches wide. Under the drawing he wrote in graffiti script, "No mas."

All items were returned to his left jacket pocket.

He looked downward toward Erica—she was 52 years old—reverently nodded, then turned to leave her home. He allowed the outside porch light to remain illuminated, and left the front and storm doors slightly ajar. The time was 5:26 p.m., a complete and moonless darkness, with the snow continuing to fall. He had been with Erica for a total of nine minutes.

Cautiously, with his keen eyes searching the landscape, he began his exit, leaving perfectly formed footprints in the freshly fallen snow. About twenty-five feet from his unlocked truck he stopped, removed his boots, and walked curbside to his pick-up. Once inside the cab, he started the vehicle, turned on the heater, changed his socks, and put on his black leather clogs. He then removed the inserted cotton balls from the boots. Seated comfortably, he turned on the windshield wipers and pulled away from his parking space. Unnoticed, he drove away from Calipso Street, turned right onto Delta Avenue, and proceeded to drive to the Level District of the city for a planned date with a woman friend at Club Zapatas for Mexican food and cerveza. On the way to Club Zapatas, as he slowly passed the Third Precinct Police Station, he reached outside his driver's side window and gently placed the pair of black work boots atop the hood of a recently parked police cruiser.

The following morning, a neighbor, walking her dog, noticed that Erica's front porch light was still turned on. Approaching her home, she also observed that the front door was not completely closed. Erica had been dead for sixteen hours.

Chapter 8

"AN ATTEMPT AT FIGURE STUDIES"

Colerain Pike and Gina Epki made arrangements to meet at Club Zapatas at 6:00 p.m. for drinks, some dinner, and later possible opportunities that evening for private time. As expected, Gina pulled her Toyota Xterra into the parking slot adjacent to his pick-up, just seconds after Colerain finished parking. Leaving his leather gloves on the passenger side front seat, he exited his vehicle into the extended, friendly arms of the spirited department store manager.

Both Gina and Colerain were absolutely elated to be in each other's company.

Gina playfully teased Colerain about his clog-type shoes by taunting him with some rapid fire comments. "Mister, it is snowy out there. Why are you wearing your Hansel and Gretel slippers tonight? Are you crazy?

Her provocative perfect smile and wise-ass commentary were always turn-ons for Colerain. Gina was thirty-eight, looked ten years younger, divorced, and drop-dead gorgeous.

She loved her position with the Redtower Department Store where she supervised six excellent assistant managers. Purchasing, pricing, buying, selling, displaying, and wearing the latest clothing fashions were among her life's passions.

Gina was always dressed impeccably with the latest fashion trends, walked like a starlet, spoke in a slightly raspy and sultry voice, yet, she was a focused businesswoman when it came to her diverse investment portfolio and her four condo properties. She loved being with Colerain. She relished his playful bad-boy image and bantered back and forth with him, sending taunts to each other about getting tired of the present company and kicking them to the curb. She thought that this Mr. Pike was handsome, athletic, took good care of himself, and artistic. She loved the fact that he never made an issue about spending money with or on her.

At Club Zapatas they ordered two ice-cold Coronas and an appetizer of rojo nacho chips with Quintana Roo brand mild salsa. They chit-chatted, canoodled, and flirted, allowing some teasingly raw language and sexual innuendos to enter into their conversation as they savored the chips, salsa, and beer. Their regular waitress, Rokie Nelson [D], who served them attentively, brought them two more Coronas and then took their orders without using a writing implement or notepad. Both relaxed diners ordered a trio of Mexican tacos, hers with chicken and Colerain with beef, that included a side of black beans and rice mash. While eating, Gina suggested to her dining companion that she might be interested in a figure-drawing session at her Elevation Avenue condominium that overlooked the snow-covered Downtown Center City.

Their meal enjoyed and the table cleared by the doting Rokie, the couple tossed down a shot of El Caballo tequila and one more bottle of their favorite cold cerveza. At this point in the conversation, Colerain indicated that he would be delighted to undertake some serious nude-figure drawing studies. His artistic skills had been present since childhood and through life he became quite adept at drawing and rendering. In reality, drawing was a comforting pleasure of his, akin to opium. Gina admitted to becoming very excited about the thought of posing in the nude for her talented artist friend. With a suppressed laugh and some youthful giggles, she related to him that she had a particular type of itch that only he could eliminate. Colerain rolled his sparkling eyes at that thought.

Colerain motioned for Ms. Nelson. She came immediately and presented him with the tab for the meal and their beverages. The ticket was for $38.75. Colerain handed her four twenty-dollar bills and told her to keep the change. Colerain's appreciation for her service was always among the most bountiful of the gratuities that she received at Zapatas.

Upon leaving the restaurant, they walked arm in arm to their vehicles and then Colerain followed Gina up the narrow and recently snow-plowed Elevation Avenue to her residence in the Witt-Oldis Towers. Yearly, she reserved and paid for two select spaces in parking facility under the eight-story structure. They parked their vehicles in the adjoining spaces, Gina leaving her Xterra unlocked and Colerain locking his Ranger. A swift and silent elevator ride whisked them to the penthouse level and they jetted into unit 812. Her condominium provided spectacular vistas with enormous sections of one-way glass lining the two window fronts facing the urban landscape. Colerain thought that her living space was richly and stylishly decorated. He loved her preferred Asian and Southwestern USA blending. One of the city's most coveted and respected decorators, Harve Haddix [E], was commissioned to decorate, with little concern for adhering to a budget to enhance her home.

Colerain stored drawing and sketching supplies and watercolor painting materials at Gina's. A drawing board, three assorted drawing tablets, sketching pencils and pens, watercolor paints, and brushes filled a large, black leather portfolio.

Gina whispered, "I can't wait to get started."

"Let's go, I am very focused and stimulated," replied Colerain.

Within seconds her clothing was removed and the nude model tossed her black skirt and sweater onto the plush carpeted floor, followed by her mini jeweled black thong. Instead of taking a posing position on a Native American woven blanket that was draped over her one-hundred-inch-long couch, she approached Colerain and brushed her apple-sized breasts against his partially opened lips. Her erect nipples and wonderfully toned, sleek body were too much of a distraction for the amateur artist who allowed his supplies to cascade onto the carpet.

An hour-long exhilarating period of lovemaking ensued that was dominated by copious amounts of passionate energy and multiple position interchanges. Colerain was able to climax twice during the hour of lovemaking. Noteworthy for a fifty-four-year-old man, he reminded himself. Gina also enjoyed the activity and position changes. She boasted of having been satisfied multiple times during the exhausting encounter. Their energy spent, both Gina and Colerain succumbed to their great desire to rest, falling asleep together under the comforting Arapahoe blanket from Colorado. Obviously, he felt most welcome to stay the night.

Chapter 9

"THE OFFERING OF FACTS AND CIRCUMSTANCES"

Officers Rob Skinner [F] and Halworth Smith [G] were leaving the Wilson Avenue Third Precinct Police Station to begin their regular patrols on the 10:00 p.m. to 6:00 a.m. watch.

Officer Skinner commented, "What's this shit?" upon seeing the pair of black work boots standing erectly upon the hood of their warming and waiting squad car.

"I wonder who put those damn things there?" added Hal Smith.

"I'll toss them into the building for now, and we better get hopping because we have an apparent murder scene to secure on Calipso Street," Officer Skinner quickly answered. Then he added softly, "A woman was strangled."

Also rushing to the scene were a pair of seasoned, veteran homicide detectives from major crime divisions. Ricardo Stuart [H] and Fredericka Green [I] had just been given the assignment to conduct the preliminary investigation of the Calipso Street homicide.

Instantly, upon her arrival, Detective Green asked the securing police officers, "What do we have, gentlemen?"

Officer Skinner responded. "We have a deceased white female apparently posed in some manner with a drawing or painting on her torso. She is in a state of complete undress, and from outward appearances she does not appear to have been sexually assaulted. But someone may have shaved her private area because there is hair stubble on the carpet in that area of her body."

"Detectives," added Rob Skinner, "it sure looks like she may have been strangled."

"Officers, will you please secure the front walkway, steps, etc.? We still have some readable footprints in the snow outside," Detective Stuart requested.

Within minutes, a police crime scene photographer arrived at the investigation site. Danielle Kravitz [J] was given permission to begin taking an array of digital photo images of the deceased woman's body from various angles and positions, including close-ups of her neck area, the drawing between her breasts, and of her pubic area.

Detective Fredericka Green asked Ms. Kravitz, a veteran of twenty-four years of photographing crime and accident scenes, "Have you ever see anything like this with the fucking artwork and such?"

"I've seen words written in blood, lipstick, and paint. I've seen re-dressing and undressing with weird and perverted body posings. And, I've photographed mutilations and abuse that I'll never forget, but I have never seen an artistic drawing and the clean pubic shaving with no other violation of the corpse," she replied in a stunned emotionless voice.

Detective Stuart stared momentarily at Fredericka and asked, "Do you see anything else that this killer could have left behind to provide us with a bit more information?"

"You know, Ricardo, I have gone over everything, multiple times, trying to call upon my instincts and relying upon my experience to see if I'm missing something. But this killer hardly moved around. Maybe remaining in an area no bigger than eight feet by eight feet in Ms. Stamcic's living room. It seems as though this person was very well prepared, acted quickly, expertly, and exited in a most timely fashion. The footprints in the snow and in the carpet might be our only physical information of this heinous visit. Besides the artwork, and something micro, I mean," Fredericka responded as she pushed her collar-length reddish-brown hair behind her triple-studded earlobes.

Chapter 10

"UNDERTAKING A JOURNEY WITHOUT FEAR"

The driving distance from the ever-expanding hub of Southwestern Pennsylvania to Louisville, Kentucky, was approximately 430 miles. The Greyhound "Scenic Cruiser" was designed to seat sixty passengers. Fifteen rows, each with double seats, balanced the left and right sides of the bus. The intersecting aisle was tight. A large or obese person would need to navigate it by walking sideways. Colerain did locate a seat, driver's side, in the middle area of the vehicle. The bus appeared to be two or three riders short of full capacity.

A lingering staleness, possibly enhanced by bleach, suggested that the conveyance may have been recently cleaned. The advertised air-conditioning was operating, but the number of passengers already dabbing at their brows was a negative indicator of its effectiveness.

Colerain initially wished that he could have occupied a window seat instead of his on the aisle. While he looked toward the window, a momentary beam of sunlight highlighted the oil or sweat blotches of the human heads that had rested there. The aisle seat would be better. The unpleasant thought of his face absorbing a stranger's sweat or grease prompted him to reflect uncomfortably upon boogers, blood, fecal stains, farts, and other human emissions. He promised himself not to touch anything as he turned to examine his seat's vinyl headrest.

He sat next to a young woman, twenty-ish, who did not speak to or acknowledge Colerain. Her long, dark, poker-straight hair was parted precisely down the middle. A liberal application of makeup, including false eyelashes, was evident upon the comely woman's face. A blue denim jacket was draped over her shoulders, allowing her tube-top-covered torso and bare midriff to be exposed. Again, he peered toward the greasy window, debating whether to warn his fellow passenger. His eyes glanced across her form and noticed a tear in her tube top, where an erect pink nipple was protruding from that opening. Instead of a siren's invitation, he somehow saw the protrusion as vulgar.

The bus driver, Walt Schuffenecker,* announced that the duration of the drive would be ten hours. He indicated that there would be required stops in Wheeling, West Virginia, Columbus, Ohio, and Cincinnati, Ohio, plus two courtesy stops at highway rest islands. Many passengers appeared to have packed bag or box lunches. Colerain did not, anticipating a possible stop at Highway Plaza. He carried twenty-two dollars, following a guideline from his military travel plans not to have too much currency in his possession.

(* Name is from a Paul Gauguin painting dated 1889)

Mr. Schuffenecker was about 5 feet 7 inches, lean, with dark hair, a moustache, and a full short cropped beard. He promised to note interesting vistas over the bus intercom and seemed to enjoy communicating with his passengers from his cockpit area. A visual command of the highway was enhanced by his ample seat cushion. On two or three occasions, he commented that providing tips to the driver was perfectly legal, also indicating that he made "only" $5.45 per hour.

Chapter 11

"FACTS MINUS THE DETAILS"

Fort Knox Reception Center. Four days. Begin acclimation to army life. Polish your two pairs of boots. Haircut, short. Deposit in provided trash barrels all weapons and pornography. Mess hall meals and procedures. Make up your bunk. Recognize rank of officers and enlisted men. No drugs, meds (without script), or marijuana. Take IQ and aptitude tests. Eyeglasses to all that need (only one style). No beards.

Basic training. Nine weeks. Early a.m. PT. Protein- and carbohydrate-loaded breakfasts. 10 minutes to eat. Smoke 'em if you got 'em (27 cents per pack). Drill and ceremony. Push-ups on DI discretion. March, attention, about face, to the rear, present arms, etc. Double time, everywhere. Barracks inspections. Lights out and silence. Fire watch duty. KP. Know your squad, platoon, and company. Trainees from everywhere. Bossier City, Louisiana, Davis, California, Cleveland, Ohio, Philadelphia, Mississippi, Rome, New York, etc. Southern, Northern, Eastern, Western. 5 feet 2 inches to 6 feet 6 inches. 18 years old to 28 years old. 125 lbs to 265 lbs. White, black, Hispanic, Asian, Native American, and mixed. Mail time=sacred. Night vision training. Bayonets. No brass, no ammo. "Not a gun, young man, it's a rifle." Map reading. Weapons. M-16. Firing ranges.

Grenades. Chain of command. More IQ and aptitude testing. M.O.S. (Military Occupation Specialty) E-1 rank. Pugil sticks. Hand-to-hand combat. Low crawl. Agility course. Basic first aid. Pushups + pushups. Shuttle run. Crab crawl. Rolling monkey bars. Sick call. Roll-call. Report. Payday. $150 per month ($127 after taxes). PX. Foot locker. You buy personal supplies. Open showers. No walls separating toilet stalls. Inhibitions evaporate. Salt tablets. Latrines. Rifle range forced marches at increasing distances. Lister bags (H2O). Opportunity to worship. Race relations lectures. Article 15. Senior drill sergeant. Company commander. Clean toilets and sinks. Always, more double time. Back sink. Intel. Trust your buddy. Follow orders. Go or no go=(testing) infantry, grunts. Vietnam. Police your area. More push-ups. Day room. Graduation.

1B, basic medic course. Six weeks. Fort Sam Houston, San Antonio, Texas. Longest bus ride. "See ya" to friends. E-2 or PFC (E-3). Stop the bleeding. Access wounds. Splints. Pressure. Dog tags. Triage. Stretcher. Vital signs. Injections. For real, 5 syringes of morphine. Helicopter evac. First aid. Fractures. Clear the airway. CPR. Locate bullet hole (entry and exit). Tourniquets. Low crawling. P-38. Rations. Get wounded out alive, 91 percent survival rate in Southeast Asia. Landing zone. Dust-off. "I need a medic." Medics, important targets of enemy.

Advance Individual Infantry Training. Twelve weeks. North Fort Polk, Louisiana. Climate, weather, and humidity similar to SE Asia. Landmines, Claymore mines. Trip wires. One-time use, shoulder-fired, disposable rocket launcher. Tracking. Surprise the enemy. Kill silently (if possible) with bayonet, strangling, or slitting. Quiet movements. Signs instead of words to communicate. Expand use of other weapons. Trained and accurate sharpshooter. Read distance, wind, elevation, etc. Locate target, in and back out quickly. Discuss actions with no one. Trust only other Special Operations team members. Usually six others. Each has a needed specialty. Decisions to be made as missions evolve. Supreme physical conditioning. No detected health concerns. Above-normal ability to focus. High level of intelligence. Prepare for isolation and limited communication with individuals in command. Quick and decisive thinking. Plan, and then plan some more . . . Part of training: four weeks as a prisoner of war in a Vietnamese-run prisoner camp. Mission, try to escape. Name, rank, and serial number. Deal with deprivation, abuse, hunger, lack of sleep, physical torture, interrogations, humiliation, etc. Lost 22 pounds. Zero body fat. Training over, now. Ready to serve.

Seventeen days R&R in Australia. Many untold stories from Down Under. No surprise: Orders for Vietnam, 365 days in country (boots on the ground). 12 total missions. 91.63 percent success rate (11/12). Except for a small number of superiors, the accomplishments are left unknown. Never discuss or describe. Forever. Return to America. Rank E-5. Discharged from required two-year military commitment at Fort Ord, California. No parades, no free meals, no welcome-home signs. Airline ticket, return to point of origin. Colerain Pike was one of almost three million who served in Vietnam.

Chapter 12

"SOMETIMES, MONEY IS WELL SPENT ON THE UNNECESSARY"

Donnie Hoak [K] had been employed at Rick Schofields [L] Footgear Station for six months. He despised his $6.25 per hour position; totally boring work, awful-looking feet, disgusting odors, and whining and complaining customers. There was no other employment available for the high school dropout, who lacked serious motivation and any other viable employment skills. He accepted and maintained the position to keep his parents from constantly reminding him how useless he was. Besides, his salary was spent entirely upon himself for entertainment, clothing, and purchases from his very dependable weedman. He existed upon what he liked to refer to as fun employment.

Occasionally, a very attractive woman customer would come into the store and he would get to enjoy some fine leg shots and a few foot touches. Just last week two beautiful young women provided him with the ultimate shoe store clerk bonanza. They were not wearing any panties, going completely commando, and they provided him with several private viewings as they tried on pair after pair of five-inch stilettos. He knew that they were so open for viewing just to get a rise out of the lowly shoe salesman. He could care less. He thought it was great to walk around with a woody most of the day at the awful Footgear Station.

Colerain Pike strolled into Schofields and began a purposeful browsing of the hundreds of choices offered for sale. He lifted and examined several pairs of expensive Italian leather boots. The store had filled with several customers and Donnie Hoak was bouncing from man to woman to parent to child and back again. Thomasina Cheney [M] had called off again, leaving Donnie to cover his shift alone for the second time in four days. He questioned, sized, located from the stockroom, fitted, and then rang up sale after sale. He had no opportunity to scan for entertainment; besides, no one appeared to provide him with any noticeable interest.

As Donnie walked quickly by to serve another customer, Colerain asked, "Do you have these in an 11 1/2?"

Donnie paused, immediately recognized the brand, Plaza Amore, and asked, "What size and color?"

Without looking at Donnie, Colerain replied, "Black, size 11 1/2."

Within two minutes Donnie returned from the shoe stock storage area carrying a gray box with the Italian leather boots. "$199.99," he stated. "Wanna try them on?"

Colerain shook his head no as he reached into his front left slacks pocket and removed 10 twenty-dollar bills. Even though Donnie was besieged by several pressing customers, he maintained a certain calmness and actually was attempting to respond to the shoppers in the order that they entered the store. He rang up Colerain's purchase, accepted the cash payment, placed the boots into a Schofield carrying bag, and slid in the receipt without making any eye contact with Colerain.

Colerain accepted the carrying bag and thought about the lightness of his package. He strode purposefully out of the shoe store without any alteration of the expression upon his face. He was thinking, business, simply business.

Colerain realized that by selecting a very busy time period at the shoe store, and by appearing to know exactly what he wanted to purchase, and by not trying on the shoes, that he would probably go unnoticed and unidentifiable. He had also selected Schofields Footgear Station because he was aware that the store had, because of the expense, delayed by three months installing video surveillance cameras on the premises.

Chapter 13

"FORTY-EIGHT DAYS IN BETWEEN"

The ongoing murder investigation of Erica Stamcic wasn't able to produce any more viable clues or information. In fact, during daily briefings the official written report of the homicide was noted only by a statement indicating that all leads were still currently being investigated. No witnesses, no traceable or pursue-able clues, no leads gleaned from Erica's telephone records, and no suspects had been brought in to be questioned or interviewed. Nothing. The murder appeared to be random, yet well timed and precisely committed.

Detectives Green and Stuart studied the photographs of the victim on numerous occasions, hoping to gain some new insight or discover some overlooked clue. The only pertinent information that they had to study was the drawing on the body, the pubic shaving, the non-violated body (not sexually violated, anyway), the death by wire strangulation, and the size 11 1/2 footprints. Their efforts had apparently reached the proverbial brick wall. Detective Fredericka Green did not believe that this killer was a man who needed to seek notoriety or attention. She feared that he would never have a need or reason to make any attempt to contact police to unburden himself in regards to his vulgar deed. That thoughtful opinion was based upon her long career in police detective work.

Erica Stamcic got along well with co-workers at Labine-Mizell [N] [O] Investments and Securities, where she held the position of office manager for the past six years. She had not fired anyone during her tenure and she had no complaints filed against her by any employee in her official capacity as manager. She socialized appropriately and it did not appear that she had a suitor or love interest among her office co-workers. Several of her neighbors, when canvassed, indicated that she was a very private woman, yet always helpful and friendly during neighborhood contacts. She had no outstanding debts, other than her home mortgage, and did not owe money to any single individual or group. She did not use illicit drugs or frequent bars or clubs, preferring the privacy of her home and small circle of family and friends. Apparently, she lacked enemies. Also, it was determined that she had no repair or remodeling work of any kind done to her home during the past thirty-six months, providing no possible suspects from workmen or estimators. The sad fact of the matter was, she was dead. Everything but the remaining thoughts of the dead seemed dead.

Chapter 14

"THE BULLETIN"

A recently printed Sunday church bulletin from St. Euphemia of the Five Wounds Parish was lying upon the cracked leather bench seat in a booth at Polly's Potluck Diner. Colerain picked up the bulletin and began to glance at its contents. It was dated January 12, 2012. He had already ordered a turkey club sandwich, a large Polish dill pickle, lite-mayonnaise on the side, and a medium diet soft drink with no ice.

Leafing through the church bulletin articles, Colerain spied an item that indicated that the parish was searching for a local volunteer to do some touch-up carpentry work on a complex wooden altar railing at St Euphemia Catholic Church. The name listed as the contact person for any interested volunteers was Jodie Brooktide. The article also supplied her home telephone number at 418-215-8817. As Colerain expected, no remuneration could be offered, but the worker would receive prayer, praise, and possible commission work from St. Euphemia.

While Colerain enjoyed his turkey club sandwich and diet beverage, he took pleasure in flirting with his waitress, a grandmotherly lady named Josie Gibbon [P]. She reminded him of someone who continued to work, well into her sixties, because of pressing economic necessity. He liked her and would tip her generously.

Colerain was able to retrieve instantaneously all of his stored information relating to Ms. Jodie Brooktide. He had dated her for two years while she taught at Lincoln Place Junior High School exactly twenty years ago. She was a member of the World Languages Department and was a highly regarded educator. Jodie was almost five months older than Colerain and she would be turning a baby booming fifty-nine on March 3, 2012.

Ms. Brooktide was an attractive, well-educated, independent, retired schoolteacher who, unless she had moved recently, resided in the Pine Heights neighborhood where St. Euphemia Catholic Church was located. Colerain and Jodie pursued each other during the two years that they were together. Their frequent exchanges grew into flirting and innuendos, where their wits were matched against one another in playful bantering. A stolen kiss here, a hand sliding up a skirt there, the short dark hair, and the lean and tight body of this woman in her mid-thirties had him thinking about her constantly. She exhibited ramrod-straight posture and a heightened level of dignity in her conduct, with the only exceptions coming when she was able to be relaxed around Colerain.

Colerain sensed that a man would have to regularly accompany her to church and meet her mother before he could entertain any thoughts of having his way with her. Jodie did admit to having carnal interest in him, but she insisted that the proper steps would have to be taken by any man who would like to have her. Even with the stated insurmountable restrictions, Jodie was firmly embedded in Colerain's head.

Colerain playfully reasoned that a virgin in her mid-thirties, who was still very desirable, could be auctioned off to the highest-bidding third-world warlord for a small fortune. He suspected that since Jodie's widowed elderly mother resided with her, the teacher was constricted and restricted by the family and moral pressures placed upon her by dear, old Mom. Colerain believed himself correct that through guilt, pressure, or other means, her mother had prevented her from becoming emancipated.

This scenario appears to be very common in many worldwide cultures. A daughter, usually the eldest, graduates from college and secures a well-paying professional position. Unfortunately, she is unable to gain independence from her family. Her father passed away several years ago from a myocardial infarction. A life of hard labor in a steel mill, cigarette smoking, and excessive alcohol consumption stole years from his lifespan. Mom, bless her heart, was the homemaker who never had to leave her comfortable suburban home to seek employment. Her beloved husband, Mickey, took good care of her and their family.

That is the way that it panned out for Jodie. She inherited the position to take care of her mother and its endless amounts of guilt. Colerain knew quite well that if Jodie's mother was still alive, she would be residing with her daughter in Pine Heights. In fact, their home was located at 1014 Comstock Road, according to the Chapman-Hayes County homeowners website. Jodie Brooktide had purchased her home in July 1990 for $105,000 with no mortgage lending company listed. Jodie owned her home outright and its November 2007 assessed value was taxed at a rate to indicate it was worth $190,000. Colerain was aware that Pine Heights was an excellent community with good schools, low crime statistics, and ever-rising property values.

From time to time, thoughts of her would dart into his mind and re-awaken a plethora of deeply seated emotions. Since reading that church bulletin, it had become nearly impossible for him to remove those thoughts from his daily conscious and waking moments.

The distances between homes on Comstock Road were generous. Ms. Brooktide's property occupied a corner lot with the green zone of an elementary school directly next to her home. Across Comstock, with approximately two hundred feet of front yard, and directly opposite from her was the nearest neighbor. The substantially sized lots of the neighborhood provided for serene privacy and extensive yard and maintenance duties. Perpendicular to Comstock was Baneberry Road where a heavily wooded area was preserved for wildlife habitation and indigenous plant reforestation.

Predictably, her two-story colonial was landscaped with splendid and dense ornamental shrubbery, with many conifer trees lining her property boundaries. A one-hundred-and-twenty-five-foot-long driveway curved in its approach to her home. The thirty-year-old structure rested upon its tabletop lot with a two-car detached garage directly to its rear. A vehicle or two could easily be parked upon the hard, dry lawn next to the driveway and could be reasonably well hidden by a stand of broad, mature blue spruce trees.

Driving to Gina's, Colerain remembered, from the church bulletin, the contact name of Willie Mae Virdon [Q]. Ms. Virdon was the church's business executive, whom everyone realized ran the day-to-day operations of St. Euphemia of the Five Wounds Parish.

Watching a wall-mounted flat screen television at the Elevation Avenue condominium, Gina and Colerain savored the Steelers smoking the Ravens by a score of 28 to 7. All four Steeler touchdowns were scored by the defense or by the special teams. Two interceptions were run back for touchdowns, as well as a fumble recovery in the opponent's end zone, and an electrifying punt return of seventy-one yards. He and Gina enjoyed the victory, then they relished and exhausted one another other. They ended up gazing through her panoramic windows at the magnificent views of the city presented into a star-filled winter night sky. Sleep came easily for Gina. By 10:00 p.m. she was sleeping comfortably as Colerain covered her with a plush down comforter and gently kissed her goodnight and goodbye. He set her alarm clock for a 5:45 a.m. Monday morning wake-up, and engaged her home alarm system to defend the premises and quietly exited the condominium.

Chapter 15

"SOYEZ AMOUREUSES VOUS SEREZ HEUREUSES"

(Be in love and you will be happy)

A dark and moonless January sky, completely lacking cloud formations, had descended over the Pine Heights neighborhood, still somewhat early at 5:15 p.m. and slightly before the spectacular winter stars begin to offer their bold displays of their shimmering facets. His vehicle was parked and hidden among the lower boughs of the massive blue spruce trees that lined Jodie's driveway. A clean approach, on grass, would permit him an opportunity to slip into the trees and shrubs if any street traffic happened by. It was possible that one of her few neighbors might be returning to their home after their day of employment. Colerain had taken into account that possibility. He knew that those employed neighbors were from the social strata that dined out on a regular basis, in particular, on an average Monday evening. There was always so much more work to catch up with at the beginning of the work week and no time for home-cooked dining.

Colerain wore his newly purchased size 11 1/2 cotton ball-stuffed black leather boots. His slacks were the preferred black Rogue brand topped by a pea green-colored cashmere pullover sweater. He also wore his black lambskin leather jacket and a pair of black leather gloves completed his stylish ensemble.

Unnoticed and unheard, he reached the front door of Jodie Brooktide's home at precisely 5:17 p.m. An ill-tempered January wind began slicing through the nearby spruce boughs, producing disturbing, moaning sounds. His gloved hand grasped then tapped the brass door knocker and two metallic-sounding taps were produced. The carriage-styled porch light cast undefined elongated shadows as Colerain kept his head tucked into his shoulder as protection against the fierce wind. Sounds from within indicated that a chain slider was engaged and that a deadbolt was unlocked.

The front door opened five inches or so, then the pleasant voice of Ms. Jodie Brooktide questioned, "May I help you?" through the opened space of the door.

"Willie Mae Virdon suggested that I make an effort to meet with you about working upon the wooden railing at St. Euphemia's. I've lost cell phone service, therefore I couldn't call you at 418-215-8817, but fortunately, I was in the neighborhood, so," he politely replied.

Jodie inquired, "Who are you, sir?"

Colerain began to introduce himself, "I'm Colerain. . . ."

"Wait a minute, didn't I use to date you when I taught at Lincoln Place Junior High? I taught World Languages and ended my career as a supervisor in the school district," Jodie enthusiastically recalled. "Oh my God! It has been at least twenty years. My, I'm so sorry. Come in, that wind is awful out there."

The chain guard was removed and Colerain stepped into the tiled floor entryway. He closed the front door with his foot, leaving it unlocked, and began following Jodie into a family room area after making a slight turn to the left.

Almost immediately, an older, screeching voice was heard above the background of a television that was playing at a very high volume level.

"Jodie, I need you, right now," the voice demanded.

Jodie answered, "All right, Mother, I'll be right with you."

As Jodie was turning around to face Colerain, he had already removed the piano wire from his right front jacket pocket. He spun her away from him and wrapped the wire around her thin and slightly elongated neck. The powerful combination of his hands and forearms began the immediate pressures that denied her the ability to breathe, speak, and struggle. The intense pressure was so crushing that she lost consciousness within thirty seconds or so. He delivered another set of powerful pulls on the wire and held that grip for another half minute as her body sagged backward against his supporting stance.

Colerain Pike commented quietly, "Jodie, the time has come to get you out of my head."

With his left arm he supported her body as he returned the wire to his right front jacket pocket. He then carefully laid her one-hundred-fifteen-pound body upon the periwinkle blue carpeting in the area behind the family room's sepia brown leather couch. He undressed Jodie quickly. Her buttoned white long-sleeved blouse, cardinal red slacks, white panties, 34A white bra, and black flat shoes were folded and neatly stacked upon an end table near the couch.

He positioned her arms to her sides and slightly opened her legs to reveal a thinning growth of dark pubic hair. Her breasts, relatively small, slipped to the sides of her upper chest. The areolas and nipples were unusually small, he thought.

From his left jacket pocket he removed a yellow Slick disposable razor, the permanent black marker, and the five highlighter pens. With the razor he shaved both sides of her pubic region and gave her the preferred bikini cut. He brushed the cut hairs aside and down into the carpeting. He brought her legs together, noting the slight flabbiness of her thighs as he positioned her for a modest presentation.

Between her petite breasts he drew, with the black permanent marker, the profile of a man with a combed-back hairstyle and shaded in some areas using the highlighter pens. The drawing on her milky white skin filled an area about eight inches high by six inches wide.

Under the drawing he wrote in graffiti-like script, "NO MAS."

He returned the razor, marker, and pens to his left jacket pocket.

Colerain glanced down at Jodie, noting the wine-colored markings upon her neck, and turned to depart. As he did, he caught sight of the digital clock on her DVD player. The time displayed was 5:26 p.m. He had spent eleven minutes with Jodie. With gloved hand, he flicked off the front entrance light, turned the doorknob, and without hearing any sound from Jodie's mother, he quietly closed the door and retraced his steps back along the spruce trees to his unlocked vehicle. Jodie was fifty-eight years old. While walking, he hoped that his footprints would survive in the periwinkle blue carpeting of her family room. He had intentionally pressed heavily into the carpet, wishing that the prints could be thought of as important evidence to the investigators.

A minute or so later, he was in his truck removing his boots and their cotton balls, then slipping into his black clogs. He started his pick-up, turned on the heater, and pulled away from his secluded parking spot without any illumination from his headlights. Leaving Comstock Road, he veered onto Baneberry and then turned on his headlamps. He was in the first bend of Baneberry Road, a quarter mile from Comstock Road, before he passed his first oncoming vehicle.

Within minutes he was driving toward the Level District on his way to the Club Zapatas. He was hungry and in the mood for some Mexican food and, maybe, a couple of cold beers. Because an overflowing Monday night football game crowd would be anticipated, the restaurant catered to them by offering special prices on appetizers and drinks. Colerain looked forward to the possibility of meeting new people and talking some football. Driving along his preferred route to the restaurant, he approached the Third Precinct Police Station and keenly surveyed the environment. Decreasing his speed, he reached outside his driver's side window and gently placed the expensive pair of size 11 1/2 black leather boots upon the hood of another conveniently parked police cruiser. They still do not have security cameras installed near these city police stations. "What are they waiting for?"

Around 6:00 a.m. the following morning, shrieks and screams from Jodie's mother aroused a neighbor who heard the wailing as she was leaving for work. Jodie had been dead for thirteen hours.

Chapter 16

"THE PUNCTUATION AT THE END OF WORDS GIVES MEANING TO THE WORDS."

Homicide detectives Green and Stuart were gently and patiently attempting to retrieve any information from the disoriented ninety-year-old Irena Brooktide. Fredericka Green spoke directly into Mrs. Brooktide's visual reference field and asked questions clearly and with greater-than-normal voice volume.

"Mrs. Brooktide, did you see or hear anything unusual or different at home last evening?" asked the detective.

The woman's response startled Fredericka. "That bitch daughter of mine didn't bring me my hot-chocolate-with-marshmallows-and-graham-cracker bedtime snack. Where the hell is that asshole daughter of mine?"

Also stunned by the abrupt and vile response, Ricardo Stuart asked, "Did anyone visit your home last evening? Did you see or hear anyone?"

The ninety-year-old replied, "I always watch the Dean Martin show. For an Eye-talian, he ain't too greasy."

The crime scene on Comstock Road was visually inspected, dusted for prints, micro-searched for fibers, etc., and photographed extensively. The nearly perfect remaining footprints (three in number) formed in the plush blue periwinkle carpet were measured and determined to be of the size 11 1/2. It was also noted that the prints were made by hard-soled and treadless footwear.

Ms. Jodie Brooktide did not appear to have been sexually assaulted. The only signs of the physical assault were the purple and blackened neck markings and the quarter-inch deep red-black indented line along her mid-throat. The body positioning, the shaving of the pubic area, and torso drawing were eerily similar to the details of the Erica Stamcic murder scene. As with Ms. Stamcic's, Jodie's clothing was neatly folded, yet nothing else in her home appeared to have been disturbed.

Two single attractive women were dead. A similar killing method or operation was used. There were no signs of a forced entry, no outstanding or revealing clues, no witnesses. There was a total lack of viable information from a neighborhood canvass, and nothing was defined to supply investigators with any solid leads.

The single, solitary clue seems to have been intentionally left at the murder scenes: the size 11 1/2 footprints in the carpet and the snow.

"Why might this person want us to know about his shoe size?" wondered Veronica Blackburn as she unintentionally played with the strands of her hair that had fallen across her bewildered face.

Immediate background checks of Jodie Brooktide's relationships were run. Former lovers, whom she dated, neighbors, family and relatives, contractors, repairman, co-workers, students of note, etc. The detectives believed that, possibly, some specific information might be uncovered to enhance and assist in the stagnating investigation.

Chapter 17

"FOUR BOOTS ON THE SAME CRUISER"

Early on the morning after the Brooktide homicide, Officer Ricky Groat [R] and his rookie partner Leroy Face [S] were leaving the Third Precinct Police Station to begin their 6:00 a.m. drive shift.

Officer Groat said to the rookie Leroy Face, "Hey Lift"—get it, "Facelift," his nickname—"someone left some expensive-looking black leather boots on the patrol car. Shit, these bad boys are size 11.5, just my size. They appear to be brand new. I might keep these brogans."

"Just throw them in the backseat and let's get riding, Ricky," the overly concerned rookie patrolman suggested.

He was being trained to do everything by the book and he didn't want to be involved in anything that could be considered receiving contraband or gaining ill-gotten goods in any manner. The boots looked too good to have been trashed. Someone was bound to be searching for them, he concluded.

Chapter 18

"OUT OF HIS HEAD?"

Colerain Pike was easily able to erase all thoughts pertaining to his actions in the deaths of Erica and Jodie. He had not derived a single scintilla of pleasure or satisfaction from taking their lives. Conversely, he was not troubled or burdened by any feelings of guilt. He harbored no inclination to share or relate to another human being his motivation or reasoning for his behavior or the commission of the killings. Unrepentantly, he pleasantly possessed an improved state of mind. Comforted that these two women were permanently removed from his head, he was sleeping soundly They were eliminated and, unfortunately for the women and their loved ones, they were dead. Colerain non-egotistically believed that he had performed his cleansing so carefully and expertly that he might never be in any position to be held accountable. Even quietly within himself, he would never permit boasting or bragging about his ability to plan and successfully perform these killing deeds. Within the recessed corners of his thoughts, he felt serenely relieved that he would never be burdened with any transient thoughts of those two women again.

With an innate ability to command his gifted capacity for instant and total recall, he could have described in detail every aspect of their appearance and form. His visual memory was so profound and he was able to recall the most obscure factoid about them. He remembered the pattern in the iris of their eyes. He was able to map the moles that randomly traversed their bodies. He recalled when their navels were cultivating tiny colonies of lint. He was able to remember conversations verbatim and details of the locations where they socialized. He could see facial expressions made twenty years ago that corresponded to those conversations. He could, but now he no longer needed to because they were permanently excised out of his head.

Unfortunately, for Colerain Avant Pike his relaxed state of mind was short-lived. Within a week or so of Ms. Brooktide's strangulation, his mind began to re-load with thoughts of two other women. They were as firmly entrenched within him as the two women who had already been removed. Again, he became unsettled and distracted. The thoughts of others, two others, rushed back to him with the regular timing of the high tides that were controlled by the gravity of our lunar neighbor. He began to replay complete scenarios and vignettes that involved both of the two women. So much about them, from physical appearance to dialogues during encounters appeared. These thoughts now compelled Colerain to face his inability to effectively remove them from his head. During these days of revived compelling thoughts, Colerain realized that he must proceed. The powerful internal directive to cleanse had reappeared more potently than at any time previously. He possessed no amount of compulsiveness to act, for he sensed that clear and convenient opportunities would need to present themselves to allow him to proceed to the next stages of his sinister mission.

Chapter 19

"THE PAST CANNOT BE PAST, BUT IT CAN BE THE PRESENT"

The twenty-one-year-old Vietnam veteran comfortably assimilated into the college environment. He appreciated the economic freedom supplied by the tuition and living expense stipends from his parents. Some lingering resentment was occasionally extended toward Colerain for his decision to "throw" away two years of his life.

His father often repeated this mantra, "Let the others do the fighting. We need to be available for more important things."

Confident yet unassuming, he cherished his place on campus and intended to pursue only the subject areas that commanded his interest. The study of physical geography and cultural anthropology became his passions. He had always been intrigued by the physical complexities of the planet Earth and their direct impact upon human environments and their development. When Colerain's father questioned his son about his major or areas of study, he always inquired sarcastically, "What are you going to do with that?"

After graduation, without attending the ceremony of pomp and circumstance, he quietly assumed a position within his father's expanding banking empire. Colerain processed, examined, and then determined if home mortgage loans were to be granted to eligible applicants. On a number of occasions he was privately chastised in the inner sanctum of his father's office suite. "Why did you grant a mortgage to this mixed couple? That black man and white woman probably won't stay together. That 42-year-old Mexican man is classified as blue collar. Did you realize that those two women applicants are probably lesbians? That twenty-eight-year-old overweight woman doesn't have the highest-earning ceiling. If any of these people default on their loans, we will lose money. Do you understand?"

Colerain's salary was $60,000 per year plus health and life insurance policies. As a bonus, he was fast-tracked to be eligible for the possible bounty of year-end bonuses. Obviously, this fortunate and substantial income was extremely rare and unusual for a man in his mid-twenties during the mid-1970s. He resided in a spacious and newly constructed condominium with a laundry, fireplace, fully equipped kitchen, and two baths. Also included was an indoor parking space for his modestly equipped Ford Maverick. Colerain enjoyed travel within the contiguous 48 United States, attending sporting events, dating selectively, and he also believed in saving 20 percent of his annual income.

Chapter 20

"UNEXPECTED DEATH BY H2O"

Colerain was thirty years old, unmarried, childless and had recently lost his parents during their rafting vacation to the headwaters of the Amazon River. Drowning in sudden torrential flooding, their bodies were battered and broken upon jagged rocks as they were violently swept down river by unrelenting currents. Piranhas, other fish, scavenging reptiles, and amphibians feasted upon their swollen bodies. The bodies were recovered after a twelve-day search and a dragging operation of the slowly receding river. Another week was needed to process the remains from Brazil to America. After they were identified officially by dental records, cremation and a private spiritual service completed their life cycles. Colerain was the sole heir to their joint estate. After the 13 percent state inheritance tax, Colerain had legally and—many would say—fortunately inherited over seven million dollars in assets, including stock holdings, bonds, property, and cash from bank accounts.

Chapter 21

"MEDIA CREDIBILITY GAPING"

Bonby Friend [T] had been employed by the *Lone Telegraph* newspaper for eighteen months. She was constantly pitching her writing skills to Joan Christopher-Wesson [U], chief of the in-depth investigation department. Joan meticulously selected the writers and their topics for in-depth and current news reporting assignments. The two currently unsolved murders had already caught the public's attention and raised the area's level of concern. Ms. Friend had done her homework and presented a persuasive case to the chief who recognized the tenacity in the budding reporter. After two days of consideration, she granted Bonby the opportunity to work on that evolving story exclusively.

Seven emails and four unanswered telephone calls to Detective Fredericka Green did not deter her. Via chance or kismet, she shared a rising elevator at city hall with the easily recognizable detective.

"Ms. Green, allow me to introduce myself. I'm Bonby Friend, an investigative reporter from the *Lone Telegraph*. I tried to contact you several times in the past few days. I would—"

"Stop right there, young lady. I heard and have read your messages. Meet me tomorrow morning at 9:00, at R Walker Clementes [V] Coffee Express, and maybe I can answer some of your questions." The elevator door opened onto the eighth floor, and the detective exited without waiting for any response.

Ms. Green was already seated, sipping on a delightful latte concoction and nibbling upon a raisin oatmeal cookie, when Bonby arrived at 8:55.

"Morning, Ms. Green. May I join you?" she announced.

"Have a seat, Miss Friend." she replied. She swiveled her head toward the counter area and called out to RC Oldis [W], the café owner, and asked, "Can you send a barista over to take an order for my guest?"

"My pleasure, Ms. Witt. Billie Rae, please take care of our important customers," he requested from his newest barista in training.

Billie Rae Mazeroski [X], nineteen and cute as a button, tentatively approached their table with an Apple iPad in hand.

"Medium dark chocolate mochaccino, please," Bonby stated without being asked.

Fredericka paused then said, "There are a number of reasons why I have decided to have an exchange with you this morning. You seem to overflow with persistence, a doggedness to get at the trail, and, I sense, an aching hunger to write, and write well. Why don't I sit back and listen while you share your thoughts?"

Bonby began, "As a woman I find it difficult and frightening to invest in studying these recent murders. But a plethora of questions besiege me. Will there be more killings? How does the killer choose the victims? Are they known or randomly selected? If there are to be more victims, will they also be white? Can women of color or other races become less concerned and less vigilant? Will any other possible targets continue to be single and childless? Will that allow the married, mothers, and grandmothers to surrender their guard? How much of the investigated details should be disseminated to the public? Why is the footwear being gifted to the police? What, if any, is the meaning of the drawings on the deceased torsos? Will the public discussing and becoming fixated upon the crimes assist or hinder the investigation? I could go on and on."

"I am impressed by the volume of your stream of questioning, yet, I wonder why you have chosen not to use any masculine pronouns in any of your queries?" commented the detective.

"I guess that I'm not sure if the killer is male or female," she replied.

"Ummm, good point," added Fredericka. "Well, Bonby, get started writing, keep me updated, and we should try to meet once a week if possible."

Chapter 22

"TRES-TROIS-DREI-TRE-TRZY-BA-THREE"

She was twenty-one and recently hired to fill the position of computer programmer for a woman who was taking a medical sabbatical to prepare for the birth of her sixth child. Wearing wheat-colored Azores jeans and a dark blue V-neck sweater, the long-term substitute was searching for room number 372B, a former storage closet converted into the computer headquarters. That tiny facility was located next office number 372A, the domain of Mr. Colerain Avant Pike.

While stepping from his office, he noticed the young woman. "Need any help?" he asked.

"I'm looking for room 372B, the computer center," she said as she held out her set of keys and a crimson folder of work information provided to all new employees.

"Welcome, you're right here," Colerain replied as he pointed toward her office entrance. "I'm Colerain, Public Investing, and I attempt to function in 372A," he said, sweeping his left hand toward his office and its wide opened door as he spoke.

She smiled, revealing brightened white teeth and an attractive face that was enhanced with a sprinkling of freckles, then introduced herself. "Hello, Colerain, I'm Anye"—pronounced awn-yea—"Santillo, and it's a pleasure to meet you."

"If you need anything, I am eager to be at your service," he responded with an engaging smile.

During those few moments of introduction, Anye was able to take a quick snapshot of Colerain, and she was quite impressed. Physically fit, handsome, mid-30s, moderately tanned, clean fingernails, casual, yet stylishly dressed, thick short hair, and she sensed that he enjoyed being around women. He possessed the "look" that she found to be excitingly attractive. Not wanting to appear too forward, she thought for a few seconds about her instantaneous attraction toward him.

She asked, "I would love to know more about your investing. Do you suppose that you would ever find some free time to show me around?"

Colerain, blessed with the natural ability of a very visual man, was also assessing his first impressions of his new co-worker. He found her pretty, possessing a body that showcased her ample breasts and carriage. The freckles on her face, arms, and upper chest had him envisioning some fun dot connecting. She comfortably looked directly into his blue-green eyes as they spoke, while he noticed her hazel-brown gems. She exuded confidence and a pervasive feminine sexuality that invited him to begin entertaining the idea of keeping company with her.

"I frequent a place nearby, very public yet comfortable, where we could stop after work," he suggested.

"I bet you do, Mister," Anye cooed. "Maybe, it's a date then."

Chapter 23

"TALENTED WOMAN, GIFTS OVERFLOWING"

The medical sabbatical would last for a period of eighteen weeks, about four and a half months. Anye and Colerain were able contain their interest in each other to some degree, although it was difficult to maintain that containment when they shared spaces less than twelve feet apart. Sealed notes delivered by trusted couriers and impromptu office visits did raise the eyebrows of some prying colleagues. Fraternization was usually frowned upon.

Her apartment or his condominium and the occasional secretive office encounter were venues that were visited to satisfy their intensifying passions. Their lovemaking was mutually gratifying with each lover taking the initiative naturally. They enjoyed each other's nakedness, with Colerain sometimes figure drawing and Anye sometimes playing her acoustic guitar and singing with her trained voice unencumbered by clothing. They seldom went out publicly, both preferring to spend the majority of their time together privately. During her final two months of employment, they resided together at her apartment, with Colerain only needing to check on his condo occasionally. Anye's one-bedroom apartment was fifteen minutes from the workplace campus. That distance reduced the opportunities for casual encounters with inquisitive colleagues.

When the sabbatical ended in early June, with Anye's contract having been successfully fulfilled, she indicated to Colerain that she felt compelled to "move on" to pursue her musical and singing career. Occasionally, she did sing back-up to some local bands. She also played a few gigs singing in piano bars, simply to cultivate her talents. Colerain often listened to her sing, and he became convinced that she had a profound level of talent. She recently met a promoter and felt comfortable knowing his business background and his interest in hiring her to travel with an alternative rock band as a backup vocalist. The band called themselves "Jagged Mouth" and had signed a six-month contract to tour America and become the opening act for several frontline groups. The promoter's homosexuality seemed to offer her comfort about traveling with a group of hard-living musicians.

Colerain politely and seriously discussed this planned undertaking with Anye. Paternally, he wanted to caution her about the perceived and relevant pitfalls that this lifestyle could hold. But he also sensed that she was already a woman of the world, confident in her abilities and ready to trust her fate as she charged into her future. When she departed, she wished him well, indicated that she would miss him dearly, never forget him, and hoped that her love for him would allow her to be near to him again someday.

It troubled him, worried him, in fact, that she proceeded without financial stability, trusting everyone and anyone, going forth into the world wherever her performing options would take her. How many other young women tossed their caution to the easily changing winds of a musical career, hoping for recognition and the rareness of success, only to be used, abused, and then cast aside and forgotten. Realistically, chances of living her dreams in the music business remained slim.

Anye had entered into Colerain's head, always to be there, always appearing and reappearing. Always in his head. Now, at this time, even after his two cleansing deeds, she was there, ever present, providing him with all of the details of their relationship. He needed to make her leave.

Chapter 24

"SUMMERTIME, AND THE LIVING IS EASY"

Colerain was paging through a local entertainment circular, humorously referred to as the *Drain*. This weekly rag listed performing bands, singers, comedians, etc., and where and when they would be performing. Gina had suggested to Colerain that they should select a local nightspot for some entertainment after dinner. They had planned to dine at Gee Cimolis [Y] Ribaris, a popular seafood emporium of the highest quality and reputation.

The *Drain* included in its listings Basils, a tavern/nightclub in the trendy city neighborhood of the Upper Reach. Basil's contained a small stage area and by charging a nominal cover charge, offered mostly unknown and cheaply booked entertainment. On this particular Saturday evening, the Jaybelles would be performing their unique brand of country soul. A photograph of the Jaybelles accompanying that information immediately caught Colerain's discerning eye. Unexpectedly, during his perusing of the group's credentials, he identified Anye, clearly a member of this all-female trio, pictured in the advertisement.

Colerain suggested Basils to Gina. She indicated that any fun venue would suffice, winking at Mr. Pike to let him know that she was really just interested in being in his company. Of course, Colerain need not disclose that he recognized a member of the performing Jaybelles. He needed to cast his eyes upon Anye. He hadn't seen her in nineteen years, and he wondered how she had maintained and provided for herself over those years. It would also be of the utmost importance that Anye would not be permitted any opportunity to catch a glance of him in the audience while she was performing.

Chapter 25

"DINNER, PLANNING AND TIME SPANNING"

Gina and Colerain arrived at Ribaris precisely on time to meet their seven-thirty reservation. They were seated at a private table toward the rear of the establishment, in close proximity to the wine steward's station. Colerain routinely sat with his back toward the wall at the rear of the restaurant, which allowed him perfect visual and sight line considerations, a necessary habit of his. Gina, as usual, was stunningly dressed. She wore a crimson red, slightly-above-the-knee, and backless evening dress. Her neckline plunged deeply enough for her to display a Polish amber necklace ensemble that Colerain had purchased for her. As was her custom, she wore no undergarments, which permitted her breasts to descend naturally and seemed to constantly project her erect nipples. Both she and her date were nervously perched at arousal's edge, knowing that she always chose not to wear anything under while in his company.

Colerain was also stylishly dressed, continental black, except for an Italian knit gaucho. The fine woolen sweater was long sleeved, Cherokee red in color, with thin white detailing at the garment's edges. Also, as was his custom, Colerain went commando.

From the menu that never listed prices, two prime swordfish steaks in a black currant sauce, rice diablo pilaf, and fresh seasonal mixed vegetables were selected. The chief wine steward always recommended the dinner wine for Colerain. Tonight he chose an ice champagne, 2001, from Isadore vineyards via California's Napa Valley. The couple enjoyed their meal immensely as evidenced by their Stazee bread swiping at empty dinner plates. Dessert was a devil's tower of chocolate Warsawa chrusciki rained upon by a blueberry-marshmallow shower. Colerain signed the credit card ticket for the amount of three hundred dollars. The actual cost of the meal was slightly under two hundred dollars. Ribaris loved Colerain and his guests, and always presented him with the finest service and considerations.

"Well, Gina, we have been fed and now, we need to be entertained," said Colerain as he looked across the table at his date.

"Dinner was sinfully good, but wouldn't you want stop somewhere for a quick sinful rendezvous?" she temptingly replied.

Colerain coyly replied, "Gina, when we take detours we are never able to get back on the track again. Besides, don't you want to hear the country soul of the Jayhawks or Blueberries or whomever they are?"

Her wide-grinned response was delivered in a barely audible whisper, "Pike let's do something in the car. I'm an addict, you know."

Chapter 26

"BASIL'S SPREADING VIRUS"

Basil's nightclub was nearly back-alley dark, completely crowded with an eclectic audience of all ages and races, besides being decorated without any reference to good taste. The name Basil's was derived from Basilava, so named for the Serbian-American woman owner. Beers were generally inexpensive and most often they were foreign imports. Colerain ordered two Pulaski Piwos and Gina requested cheese on pretzel cubes. The waitress told her "to get the fuck outta here."

The packed nightclub was easily over the 150-occupant capacity listed on the city ordinance that was unceremoniously posted above the glistening black-cherry wood bar. As it turned out, the ten-dollar-per-person cover charge entitled each customer to two complimentary beers from the impressive brew list. Patrons came for a cheap night out, some beers, and the free buffalo wings to be delivered at the entertainment's intermission.

Without warning, all of the house lights dimmed, descending the audience into an all-encompassing, slightly unnerving darkness. Only the red-orange glowing tips of dozens of simmering cigarettes, like the beady eyes of an undulating beast, highlighted the club's physical features with minimal definition.

Four house spotlights dramatically lit the stage area, demanding focus and silence from the overflowing audience. A short, slightly balding, man with a fake tan stepped to center stage. Grasping a handheld wireless mike, he sarcastically thanked the squawking audience for being in attendance.

Without warning, he boldly bellowed, "Let's welcome the Jaaaay-belllllllllles. These ladies can sing their asses off!"

The Jaybelles walked onto the stage to a smattering and sprinkling of applause from the less-than-enthusiastic audience. The three women, each appearing to be in her early forties, of equal height, and all with long and flowing dark hair, smiled at the gathering as they positioned themselves at center stage.

Their three voices rang out in unison, "Ladies and gentleman, we are the Jaybelles, we are Sasha, Anye, and Callie."

Anye, although still very pretty, possessed some noticeable facial lines around her eyes and mouth that could have indicated some hard journeys during her chosen career. Her body appeared to be fit and trim. The tight blue jeans and white cotton top allowed Colerain to take immediate notice of her still attractive feminine form. No rings were displayed upon her fingers, and her three-inch golden colored hoop earrings were her only outward indications of jewelry.

Anye had been married a total of four times. The longest of the four lasted for only two and a half years. Her first marriage was to a manager/agent who pilfered much of her earnings and physically beat her whenever she questioned, complained, or attempted to deny him physical pleasure. Marriage number two was to a talented guitarist who became a crystal meth and oxycontin addict. She remained married to Sledge, the guitarist, for seven explosive months. Her third marriage was to a singer-songwriter from Normal, Illinois, who happened to be African American. During their one-and-a-half-year union, they never had sexual relations. But fortunately, for Anye, he was kind to her and provided her with safe and calming company. He passed away from complications from AIDS. For most of his adult life, he was a down-low brother who relished his lifestyle and the multiple partners that came with it. He cared enough about Anye not to present her with any opportunity to acquire that devastating "slim" disease. Her final marriage ended two years ago when she divorced her fourth husband of fifteen months as he resided in California's Soledad prison. He was convicted of manslaughter for killing a relative over a debt of three hundred dollars. For that heartless deed, he was sentenced to a minimum of fifteen years without a chance of parole.

Anye's choices in marriage ultimately proved to be horrendous and were ill advised, but somehow of the necessary variety. She needed to be protected and treated fairly, but the nature of her business didn't offer viable alternatives. She chose to enter a very selfish and self-promoted world and too often she paid dearly for her marital or relationship decision making.

Back in their day, Colerain felt compelled to caution and protect Anye from the trials and tribulations that are commonly thrust upon individuals in the entertainment industry. Unfortunately, he was unable to. She needed to follow her aspirations and her dreams. How many other young people, men and women, chose that difficult path and endured similar challenges and difficulties as Anye? Detailed preparation, sound advice, and readily available support should be in place before any individual ventures into that complex arena of life. Someone once said, "People gotta do what people gotta do." Anye did just that.

Chapter 27

"STALLED PERFORMANCE"

Callie Foiles began to address the increasingly attentive audience. "Thank you all for coming out to see us tonight. We are pleased to be right here at Basil's, and proud to be back in this part of the United States of America. As you might know, we do our very best to uniquely cover many well-known songs from many different musical directions. Oh, and by the way, we have just recently completed recording our first CD of some of the Jaybelles' favorite selections. If you are interested, we will have that CD, titled *Three Come Calling*, for sale at ten dollars, immediately after our performance."

Callie glanced over at Anye Santillo and Sandy Burton and asked, "Are you ready to kick it up, ladies?"

Sandy was bent over at the waist with her left hand desperately gripping the edge of the three-foot-tall stool she was sitting upon. She had rather carelessly set down her Gibson traveler acoustic guitar on the stage floor at her feet. Her face was ghostly ashen and devoid of color as it was being contorted with a slightly open mouth and tightly closed eyes.

"Sandy, what's wrong?" questioned Anye as she approached her obviously stricken bandmate and placed a comforting hand upon her right shoulder.

"I have gas pains so bad that I really have to get to the bathroom," she whispered.

Callie emphatically gestured for Basilava to come up to the stage front. She continued to wave her hand in roundhouse, sweeping circles, and Basilava quickened her pace to the performing platform.

"What's going on? Is she sick?" bellowed a beefy bull of a man who was sitting at a front row table.

"Smells like dogshit up there," barked an obese red-faced woman at an adjoining table.

Basilava waved her hands in a hold-up-there-a-minute gesture. There were some low murmurings from the audience, but for the most part, the vast majority of patrons appeared to be concerned about the entertainer.

The large red-faced woman, who easily weighed some two hundred fifty pounds or more, whined about getting her money back. She was so rotund in her five-foot-three-inch frame that she was literally trying to escape from her clothing. Orange capri pants and a white tank top were bursting at their seams, pleading for her pink flesh to be set free. Remarkably, she had an image of a small red rose tattooed just above her swollen right ankle. Could she possibly believe that her skin art was helping to make her more attractive?

As Basilava conferred with the trio of entertainers, she was able to process the information about the failed start of their performance. She turned to face the audience with the cordless microphone in her heavily ringed left hand.

"Folks," she said, "a virus has gotten hold of one of our ladies, and we are hoping that it will be of the twenty-four-hour variety. Anyway, the Jaybelles will be back on our stage tomorrow evening at eight o'clock sharp. There will be no extra cover charge and everyone will get one specialty beer on the house, plus a free nacho platter. We hope to see you all again tomorrow."

As expected, there were some moans and groans from the disappointed audience. The red-faced woman, in particular, bitched about getting a refund as the opening announcer approached the stage area.

He glared at her and emphatically stated, "Why don't you shut the hell up and get your big fat ass out of here?"

Callie was given the microphone from Basilava and she directed a few final comments to the departing patronage. "We are so sorry about this evening. I know that Sandy will get a good night's rest and will be ready to go at it again tomorrow. We can't wait to get to our rooms at the Confluence Comfort Lodge and get ourselves healed and rested. Hopefully we will see you all again tomorrow. Thanks, and bye-bye."

Chapter 28

"ONLINE"

Colerain drove Gina home. She had informed him earlier during the evening that she was flying to Chicago the following morning for a regional meeting of Redtower's store managers. Her Southwest Airlines fight was scheduled to depart at 7:15 a.m. for the one-hour jaunt to Midway International and then a quick cab ride to Redtower headquarters on Lake Michigan's Gold Coast. The meeting would be conducted by the Redtower CEO, Angus Blythe, and it would begin promptly at 9:00 a.m.

They kissed. Gina commented about hating the idea of her not taking advantage of Colerain. But this was a most important quarterly meeting and she needed to get packed and sleep well to be at the top of her game.

"Night, honey," said Colerain. "Call me when you get back later tomorrow."

"I will, I'll miss you, my love," she answered.

He waited until his woman was inside her condo, saw her signal that she was safe, and indicated to him that she had armed her security system.

While driving home he allowed his thoughts of Gina to recede while he brought into clear and vivid view those of Anye Santillo.

Anye entered his head, and continuous scenes and vignettes with her began to replay in streams with vivid detail.

During this point in time, Colerain was entirely submissive to these thoughts and was decidedly unable to dismiss them.

When he pulled into his parking space, he did not exit his vehicle. Instead, he opened his laptop computer (his garage had Wi-Fi service), went to the Google search engine site, and typed in the words "Confluence Comfort Lodge" in lowercase letters. Within seconds the website for the hotel revealed itself. Colerain typed in "front881c" as the password when prompted, for hotel management access. Approximately two months before, he waited in the Confluence lobby for an out-of-town friend, who happened to be staying at the hotel. While standing near the hotel's front desk, Colerain overheard a management trainee recite that password. The young man was being trained in the reservation and placement mode used by the facility. Intuitively, Colerain stored that coded information in his memory bank, never knowing if it would ever have any viable use for him.

He was into the hotel system (change your passwords regularly, you dumb asses, he thought) and he made a quick check on the current guest listings. He entered the name Santillo and was given immediate information about the accommodations for Santillo, Anye. She was in room 101, non-smoking, queen-size bed, kitchenette, with online accessibility. By referring to the lodge's fire evacuation diagram, he noted that room 101 was located on the ground level, the last room at the end of a lengthy hallway, and nearest to the rear exit doors of that particular wing of the hotel. Since that particular room was situated on ground level, near an exit, at some distance from the elevators, and at the back end of the building, there would be far less foot traffic in that area. The parking lot and exit driving lane also would have less activity at that end of the hotel campus. He internally questioned the management of the Confluence for not realizing that they were choosing an isolated location as the accommodation for a single woman.

Chapter 29

"HIS HEAD"

Maybe it was a strain of pathetic neediness or an innate inability to deal with the realities of separation or rejection by women that compelled Colerain to act upon his decisions in regard to the women in his head. Why did this internal presence of a handful of lost loves need to be extinguished? Colerain could never get these woman back, and quite honestly, he didn't want them back into his life. He had no desire to live with or be with these women. He could never love any of the women who slipped easily in and out of his thoughts and visual recall. As the years passed, he made no attempts to keep in touch or communicate with these women. Yet, they remained cemented in his head.

Two of them are now deceased, murdered in a carefully planned ritual, that lowered by two the number of women affecting him. Anye and another woman remain. Unfortunately for Colerain, they each occupied 50 percent of his thoughts and their effect upon him remained powerful and unyielding.

Gina Epki was educated, attractive, professionally motivated, and sexually satisfying for Colerain. She adored him and secretly wished that someday he would be willing to ask for her hand in marriage. Colerain, although always aware of the talents of other women, had no current interest in being with any other woman instead of Gina. Protectively, Gina had never entered or been permitted to access the inner sanctuary of his head.

Occasionally, he thinks of the love that he freely gave to those four women. He rationalized that he was not responsible for the break-ups or separations from them. He detested those rejections. He despised the abandonment that he endured. He had always acted in a socially acceptable and dignified manner at the break-ups. He was dismissed and would never allow indications of anger, sorrow, or wounding to surface. He realized that he possessed a sizable alpha ego, and he demanded from himself that no weaknesses would ever be placed on display for others to recognize and judge.

At the time of his rejection by Erica, he silently blamed her mother. That is the conniving bitch he despised. During that painful period he had a fleeting thought of eviscerating that woman as Jack the Ripper had done to those London prostitutes.

The situation with Jodie was very different. She was from a generation where ethnic, religious, and moral ties were so powerfully binding that a son or daughter could be trapped into perpetual care for an aging or manipulative parent. That form of pressure was delivered by the powers of guilt that fell upon the back of the eldest offspring. Jodie's place at birth. Colerain did realize that Jodie's life with Mom after Papa's death must have been extremely difficult and challenging. In some strange way, maybe, he may have done her a favor. That deliverance and use of guilt to control a child should earn her mother an eternity within the inner circle of hell reserved for the damned.

Anye was the daughter of a free-spirited, unmarried, and mobile couple of the 1960s. Home was destined to be many places and the lack of a solid base proved to be the foundation for confusion. Music, travel, weed, and an attitude of "whatever, we will be okay," governed her informative years. Her parents instilled in her a zest for life without the necessary fabric, structure, and roots. She had used and enjoyed Colerain. He gave himself completely to her and was consumed by her talents and beauty. When she knew it was time for her to move on, he was discarded. Yes, discarded, as her tears flowed and voice trembled, she performed her finest act toward Colerain. A night of fabulous lovemaking.

Colerain was already plotting and directing his thoughts for her demise. The situation was very different from the others; possibly much more public and risky. Circumstances are different, yet the intended result would have to be exactly the same.

Chapter 30

"ROOM 101, NEAR THE EXIT"

Two weeks earlier, Colerain had selected a pair of black Docksider deck shoes, size 11 1/2, from a large wire basket that had been placed in the men's locker room at the Powerland Athletic Club. The club had requested that members donate usable and gently worn clothing to be made available to families from several communities that were devastated by recent spring flooding. A week ago, Colerain had brought into the club two large plastic bags overflowing with clothing items for the disaster relief drive. Included in his donations were cashmere pullover sweaters, one wheat-colored and the other pea green colored.

Of course, Colerain had made certain that his selection of the Docksiders had been made with complete discretion so that no other member was witness to his actions. Powerland Athletic Club had well over three hundred regular members and their generous donations filled the baskets and bins, which necessitated them being emptied every two days during the relief drive. Easily, dozens of pairs of footwear had been included in the offerings, which permitted a wide array of choices for his need.

The Confluence Comfort Lodge had been in continuous operation for over eighty years. It was constructed during the mid-1930s in a grand style that relied upon cut sandstone and granite, marble flooring, and slate roofing. Master Italian stone masons had been imported from Genoa, Italy, to craft the magnificent structure. The Confluence was now slowly and, at great expense, moving toward the expected standards of the twenty-first century. A complete upgrading of the air-conditioning system, whirlpool, and spa facilities for the bathroom chambers, flat screen televisions for every one of the seventy-five guest rooms, and kitchenette amenities had cost the hotel millions. Internet access and expanded entertainment cabling had also been recently installed in all rooms and suites. Currently, a $1,200,000 security and monitoring system was nearly up and running. The security company, All Seeing Eyes, had promised an April 15, 2012, completion date. Today's date was March 31, with only fifteen more days until visual security would be in effect.

The lodge was located in the Ville Mesa section of the city. The area was home to hospital complexes, research facilities, and the sprawling campus of Summit University. This densely crowded and bustling urban neighborhood was populated with shops, stores, restaurants, bars, clubs, and various businesses. Colerain happened upon a parking spot about four blocks away from the Confluence and fed the parking meter with eight quarters to guarantee himself four hours of Ville Mesa parking. Leaving his vehicle unlocked, he joined the hundreds of city workers, students, and shoppers walking upon its well-traveled sidewalks.

His six-minute stroll brought him to the fire exit lane at the rear of the landmark Confluence Lodge. As he had hoped and suspected, the hotel's rear entrance glass door had been left unlocked. Some careless guest had not taken the two extra seconds to determine if the door had been properly secured behind them. Colerain felt fortunate that he wouldn't have to use and then dispose of his universal lock probe that resembled an United States Army P-38 multiple-use K-ration can opener.

He walked into the hallway, past the ice-maker and vending machines alcove, and noted the out-of-order sign taped to the ice maker bin. The first guestroom on his right was room 101.

Colerain wore black Rogue brand slacks that barely covered the tops of his cotton ball-filled black, size 11/2 Docksider shoes. A lightweight black lambskin leather jacket worn on top of a mauve-colored silk T-shirt and the recently donned black leather gloves completed his dress ensemble. As he approached the door to room

101, it was impossible not to be affected by the sheer volume of the pulsating music emanating from within.

"In the white room, with dark curtains, at the . . ." That would be "Cream," Colerain thought to himself.

A quick backward glance did not reveal any corridor or hallway traffic. The ubiquitous maid cart was also not to be seen. He peeked at his wristwatch, mentally marking the time at 1:07 p.m. He rapped twice upon the sturdy and paneled oaken door.

"I'm coming, be right there." Anye's sweet voice immediately chimed.

Without asking who might be there or without using any security device, she freely opened the door to room 101.

Startled by her instantaneous recognition of Colerain Pike, she stammered, "Oh my God . . . Colerain . . . please come in, come in . . . let me turn down my CD player."

She was clothed in the hotel's standard white terry cloth bathrobe. Her long dark hair was wet and combed straight back and pushed behind her slightly protruding ears. Anye had just finished showering. It was obvious to Colerain that she had been able to maintain her level of attractiveness over the past two decades or so. He pushed the oaken door closed with his left foot and stepped into the foyer of the hotel suite.

Anye instinctively turned to the blaring CD player as Colerain, with wire already removed from his right front jacket pocket, wrapped the device around her neck. She attempted to speak, but no word was able to escape from her now horrified and gaping mouth. He drew the wire more tightly around her neck with a second more powerful pull. Her comely head was yanked immediately backward toward Colerain, while he inserted his right knee into her lower back as a brace to prevent her one-hundred-thirty-five-pound body from collapsing. A third sustained pull upon the wire and Anye's body fell limply against his planted leg and knee. He maintained his pressure for another thirty seconds until he experienced the extreme burning of the musculature of his hands and forearms. He released the wire's tension, loosened, and removed it from the woman's neck and returned it to his right jacket pocket.

He gently laid her lifeless body upon the light gray commercial carpeting. The carpet was plush and had been recently installed, and it continued to emit that distinctive odor of newness. Her body lay between the foot of the unmade queen-size bed and the standard hotel room dresser. As the music continued to pulsate, Colerain removed her white terry cloth bathrobe. He folded it neatly and placed it upon the bed.

Anye was completely nude. He positioned her arms to her sides and slightly opened her legs to reveal a freshly shaven pubic area. Her breasts, ample in size, had slipped to the sides of her mid-upper chest. Her medium brown-colored nipples, no longer erect, were centered in her half-dollar-sized areolas. Colerain had no need for the Slick yellow disposable shaver.

He removed the black permanent marker from his left jacket pocket and drew upon her pubic mound. He drew curly lines to imitate pubic hair in the bikini cut style that he preferred. Between her rounded breasts, he drew with the same marker pen the profile of a man with short hair and a closely trimmed goatee. Then, he shaded in some areas with the highlighter and multi-color marking pens.

Underneath the eight-by-six-inch drawing, he signed in a graffiti script the words "No mas."

All drawing items were returned to their original jacket pockets.

Colerain gazed momentarily upon the carefully positioned body of Anye Santillo and mouthed the words, "Now, you are out of my head." Anye was forty years old.

As he had done previously, he made sure to provide the expected investigators with perfectly clear shoeprints into the gray carpeting. Silently, he turned to depart. Opening the unlocked door to room 101 with gloved hand, he briefly glanced at his watch and read the time at 1:17 p.m. He had been with Anye for ten minutes. Peering into the hallway and observing its emptiness, he closed the automatically outward-locking door and departed the hotel through the glass door of the rear entrance. He decided to leave that door unsecured.

At a casual walking pace he returned to his pick-up truck and climbed in through the unlocked driver's side door. He slipped out of his purloined Docksiders and removed the cotton balls from within. He fired up his vehicle and calmly pulled out of the parking space, hoping that the next commuter would appreciate the free three and one-half hours of a prime parking space. He planned to make the size 11 1/2 shoes his latest gift to the guardians of the city. The opportunity for a delivery would just have to present itself as it had done previously.

He drove for about four or five blocks when traffic unexpectedly slowed to a snail's pace, then stopped. Several police cruisers, with roof lights flashing, were pulled over randomly at an intersection just up ahead of him. All traffic was at a complete standstill. Motorists began turning off their ignitions, consenting to the conditions. Some began exiting their vehicles and walking toward what appeared to be some form of public protest. Colerain joined the rubber-neckers walking toward the mid-afternoon media circus. He observed cameras, news media personnel, and peace officers already converging upon the intersection. Walking with the Docksiders discreetly at his side, he placed them upon the trunk of a police cruiser most distant from the activities. Knowing that the vehicles were equipped with constantly running video cameras always mounted to film in a forward manner, he selected the police vehicle's trunk farthest from the action, knowing there would be no video reference. His shoe placement also went unnoticed by the other converging motorists because all eyes were cast upon the spectacle that was unfolding.

A young woman, wearing only black and orange painted stripes, was apparently protesting the unethical treatment of animals in laboratories that tested cosmetics upon the skins of mammals. Colerain enjoyed the antics of the protester who had chained herself to a light pole and a trash receptacle. Her nakedness and attractiveness had cameras rolling and cell phones clicking, taking photos at maximum capacity and speed.

The protester's chains of self-imposed bondage were cut and removed while she was covered by a blanket, then whisked into the backseat of a police car by two female officers.

"Okay, folks, the show is over. Please return to your vehicles. We need to clear this traffic nightmare," barked a police sergeant with a broad smile radiating from his face.

Colerain joined the dozens of other motorists walking back to their vehicles. Within minutes he was in the middle of his drive back home.

Back at the Confluence, several complaints about continuous loud music from other guests alerted management. After calling then knocking and shouting, the Confluence hotel manager and a security officer entered room 101. Anye had been dead for four hours.

Chapter 31

"AT THE CONFLUENCE"

Homicide detectives Green and Stuart had just completed their required investigative paperwork on a drive-by shooting that had occurred last evening near the Kennedy Manor public housing complex. A twenty-two-year-old African-American male had been riddled with hollow point bullets from a nine-millimeter handgun. Even though some thirty to forty people were in the immediate vicinity of the shooting, the police canvass produced no viable information to assist in their investigation. Basically, a dark-colored, late-model SUV slowly drove by a group of people congregating near the entrance to a popular social club. The unidentified shooter opened fire from the front seat passenger window. Fortunately, no one other than the intended victim was injured.

The Kennedy Manor neighborhood is known to have three organized groups of young men who offer a variety of narcotics for sale. Marijuana, crack cocaine, and ten-dollar stamp bags of heroin always seem to be available for a steady stream of customers. Recent narcotics squad estimates indicated that approximately 70 percent of the illegal drug purchases were made by white suburbanites. The profits were considerable for the young black entrepreneurs. Any individual who stole money or drugs, didn't pay a related debt, sold their wares in another group's territory, or who chose to disrespect another in violation of street cred or code would commonly become the next casualty of this chosen lifestyle.

What usually occurs when police investigate this type of killing is that most people who are canvassed or questioned as potential witnesses have seen nothing. The penalty for cooperating with an investigation can be a death sentence for the witness or possible death or harm to family members or loved ones. The fear and behaviors seem little different than fears exhibited when Italian families, or mafia, controlled many aspects of their communities during earlier decades in urban American history.

Too often, many in society, including government and law enforcement officials of all races and backgrounds, see the young men killed in drug/gang activities as expendable. Undereducated and, possibly, unwilling to contribute to the betterment of society, these young men kill and get killed as society moves forward. They become expendable, some are imprisoned, some die and are buried, and many are simply forgotten.

Officer Stuart had just signed off on the forms for the drive-by shooting when he took a call from the command control dispatcher. Possible homicide, white female, Confluence Comfort Lodge, was the context of the message. Two uniformed officers already at the scene began the securing process and a preliminary canvass of lodge guests and employees.

Since detectives Green and Stuart were immediately assigned to this case, they both experienced a sickening sensation that this death might be related to the two previously unsolved strangulations. Their gut feelings proved to be entirely correct as they entered the foyer of room 101 at the Confluence Comfort Lodge.

Fredericka Green didn't have to ask too many questions of the securing officers other than the identification of the victim. The purplish bruising and the strangulation marks on the woman's neck, the placement of the body, and the drawing were obvious to her. Both she and Detective Stuart were somewhat surprised to see the differences of the drawings on this victim's body from the previous two women.

"Ricardo, did you see this?" she asked.

Stuart replied, "Yes, he drew on her pubic hair because she was shaven and the hairstyle drawn on the man's profile is shorter than on the previous drawings. Maybe, some kind of hairstyle progression. You know, first, long, then combed back, and now shorter. Maybe he is changing his appearance for each killing. And"—he added—"the 'no mas' is still there."

"No sexual violation appears to have taken place, and look, this bastard continues to leave some perfect footprints in the carpeting," Veronica commented in a voice obviously fueled by her anger and frustration.

"What kind of sick, plotting mother-fucker are we dealing with?" he responded.

"Dust everything. I want photos taken from every angle, micro check for fibers, hair, skin, everything. Check her fingernails. We can't overlook or forget anything," commanded Fredericka in a rapid deluge of orders.

Chapter 32

"LOOKING AT THE THREE"

Conference room B-3 was filled to capacity. Police Commander Gregor V. Wallace had called for a current status presentation and a skull session in reference to the three unsolved—and now officially related—strangulation murders. Charts, maps, photos, handwritten details, and descriptive information were all mounted upon the cork-lined front wall of the meeting facility.

All involved officers, detectives and investigators, forensic experts, and department specialists were required to be in attendance. Many of the individuals of note were already seated. The commander would not tolerate any tardiness. Hot coffee or tea, along with an assortment of pastries from a local neighborhood bakery, had been provided for the forty invitees.

Promptly at 8:30 a.m., Commander Wallace asked for and received the attention of the gathering.

He began. "First, I would like to make an announcement and ask for a moment of silence for a young newspaper reporter who had recently began some investigative reporting on these cases for the *Lone Telegraph*. The young lady, Bonby Friend, was killed last evening in a horrific auto accident apparently caused by a drunk driver on

Route 37 North. May our dear Lord have mercy on her soul and upon the members of her family."

The attendees held the silence until the commander proceeded with his first question. "Officer Tyler, what can you tell us about the locations of these murders?"

Billy Tyler was an expert on the physical geography of the city. He knew his city inside and out. He possessed twenty-five years' worth of detailed knowledge about every city neighborhood: their avenues, streets, alleyways, their parks, playgrounds and public property, and its commercial enterprises. If it was in the city, he made a point of studying and getting to know about its features and details.

As Officer Tyler pointed to the large and magnified city map that was mounted upon the cork wall, he stated, "The three red stars indicate the murder scenes. They are also numbered one, two, or three to indicate their order in the sequence. Three different neighborhoods with no major highway access. Also, all three areas are well known for their low crime statistics." He also added, "Geographically and spatially I have not been able to determine any links or connections to the murder sites. They appear to be randomly selected or possibly very specifically chosen by the individual committing these crimes. It is my professional opinion that this killer may have known his victims and is very comfortable in these areas of our fair metropolis."

"Thank you, Officer Tyler," Commander Wallace commented. "Any questions or reactions to or about the three murder locations?" He prompted the gathering. No questions or comments were brought forth from the attentive audience.

"Detective Green, what can you tell us about the three victims?" he said as he turned to the veteran policewoman sitting in the first row, directly in front of him.

Fredericka had received a phone call last evening from Joan Christopher Wesson informing her of Ms. Friend's sudden death. She endured a sleepless night, needed to contact Bonby's family, if possible, and visit to pay her last respects. Although shaken, she began to read from a typewritten column of outlined notes:

"Each woman was a white female. Erica Stamcic, age fifty-two, unmarried, lived alone.

"Jodie Brooktide, age fifty-eight unmarried, lived with an elderly mother.

"Anye Santillo, age forty, currently unmarried, four previous marriages. She was an entertainer, musician, no permanent residence.

"Each woman appeared to have taken good care of herself physically, and all three would be considered attractive in appearance.

"All died by manual strangulation.

"All were posed in death in the same exact positioning.

"All were either shaved or drawn upon in their pubic area to display a bikini or Brazilian style of their pubic hair.

"A profile of a man was drawn on their chest area with black and color highlight markers. The hairstyle of the profiled man was different with each successive victim, from long-haired to combed-back hair, to a shorter hairstyle.

"And please, everyone, take a very close look at the photographs displayed on the front wall boards. Maybe you might see something in the body presentation or some other detail that we didn't notice or take into account."

She continued, "As far as we can determine, these three women did not know one another. We interviewed family members, co-workers, and neighbors and the only connection that we have been able to link to these women seems to be that they were murdered by the same perpetrator."

"Detective Green," Commander Wallace said, speaking directly to the gathering.

"Yes," she answered.

"Do you believe that this killer knew these women, or that he randomly selected them for some unknown reason?" he asked.

"Random selection, absolutely not," she emphatically responded. "He knew these ladies and he knew them quite well."

"Questions for the detective?" he suggested to all in attendance. None were asked.

"Detective Stuart, what can you relate to us about the drawings, wordage, and whatever else he might have done to the bodies of the victims?" the commander asked the next investigating detective as he moved the proceedings along at a pace that was a hallmark of his time-management style."

Ricardo replied, "The drawings were done with a noticeable amount of skill. The profiles were drawn by an artist or someone with developed linear drawing ability. The 'no mas,' Spanish for 'no more,' was drawn in a graffiti style that can be commonly seen in parts of our fair city. You know, the kind of paint spraying that vandal/artists leave for the Department of Public Works to clean. Might this indicate a younger person, say, under thirty, as the murderer? I don't know. The drawing of the bikini-cut pubic hair on the shaved woman might be a need of his to keep things in perfect order. Strange that he trimmed the pubic hair of the first two women. A very odd and, possibly, revealing preference.

"There are many recorded cases where there are instances when bodies were written upon with blood, lipstick, etc. Carving words into a body is also sometimes seen. This defiling may be an attempt to make a statement, comment, or deliver some type of message. These actions appear to be well planned along with being neatly applied and deftly elaborate."

"Any questions for Detective Stuart?" questioned the commander.

"Well then, let's move forward to the evidence gathered from the murder scenes. Detective Franklin Oceak, from crime scenes, will you please address this gathering?"

"I'd be happy to, Commander," answered the veteran detective who had over thirty years of expertise in examining venues where homicides had been committed. "Basically, these three murder locations might be described as pristine. No apparent signs of struggle. No broken or displaced furniture, lamps, etc. There were no detected bloodstains, no seminal fluid, no saliva, really nothing produced by a human body, except for the trimmed pieces of the first two victims' pubic hair. We dusted extensively and found only the fingerprints of the women. The only relevant clues appear to be the footprints in the carpeting at all three sites and the boot prints in the snow outside the Stamcic home."

"What can you tell us about the footprints, Franklin?" asked the commander, as he glanced at his jeweled wristwatch. The timepiece was presented to him in recognition of thirty years of dedicated service.

"Well, sir, size 11 1/2 footprints were found at all three scenes. At scene number one, work boots with a common tread pattern. Scene two, smooth sole and heels. Probably some style of dress shoes or boot. And at murder scene three, what I call comfort shoes, like Docksiders or something like that, that had a minimal tread line."

"Thank you, Officer Oceak. Questions?" Wallace asked.

"No questions. Officer Leroy Face, will you tell us about the three pairs of 'gifts' that the police department has received since these murders have taken place?" he continued.

"Yes, sir," the slightly nervous patrolman answered. "The morning after the Brooktide homicide, my partner, Ricky Groat, and I were beginning the 6 a.m. drive shift when we noticed a pair of black boots standing upon the hood of our patrol vehicle. I picked up the boots, noticing that they were made from a fine caliber of leather, and checked the size. I was slightly pleased to see that they were size 11 1/2, just my size. I commented that I might keep them. I tossed them into the backseat and we began our patrol. While we were riding, Officer Groat mentioned that another officer, a friend of his named Rob Skinner, told him about a pair of black work boots that Skinner and his partner found on their cruiser one morning covered with snow."

Commander Wallace interrupted the patrolman, "Do you know the exact date that those work boots were found?"

"Yes," Leroy replied. "They were found the morning after the first murder, the Stamcic murder." He then added, "Recently, after the Santillo murder, a third pair, size 11/2 Docksider-styled shoes, were left upon a police vehicle the afternoon of the third murder in the vicinity of the animal treatment protest, which was approximately five blocks from the Confluence Comfort Lodge where the next murder took place."

"Officer, can you provide us with any more information about these shoe gifts, as you call them?" Wallace asked as he interrupted the presenter.

Leroy Face responded, "Well, the black work boots and the Docksiders were slightly worn on their soles and they are the type of footwear that are very common and probably sold everywhere. Now, the black dress boots appeared to be brand new and hardly ever worn. That style of footwear is sold at more exclusive shoe stores. We have seven stores in the metropolitan area that carry that particular brand and style of dress boot. Fifty-one pairs of those boots have been sold at those stores since they were introduced four months ago.

"Thirty-one of those purchases were made by credit or debit card, and the other twenty were cash sales. External Affairs is currently looking into those card purchases. So far, no good leads have evolved. Of the cash buys, eleven were recorded on store surveillance cameras. None of those eleven purchasers is considered as a suspect at this time."

"Any prints on the three pairs of 'gift' shoes?" asked Wallace.

"No sir, they were clean except for the prints of the officers or personnel who handled them," replied Officer Face.

"Anything to add? Further questions?" added the commander. "Nobody. Folks, let's get this monster before he slithers out and strikes again. Dismissed."

Chapter 33

"SOCIAL INTERACTION"

Colerain decided to stop at the local Dismal Diner to enjoy some lunch. He was in the mood for a potato pancake reuben sandwich and a plate of curly, sweet potato fries. The sandwich contained the basic reuben features that were deftly secured between two potato pancakes instead of rye or other bread. Raspberry iced tea, with Splenda, and only a few ice cubes topped off his lunch.

At the table, across and to the right of him, two women were enjoying the Dismal Diner specialty of the house; steak salads. They were unknowingly drawing attention to themselves by the occasional use of the word "fuck" or one of its derivatives. One of the woman began to weep as she related to her friend about the arrest of her seventeen-year-old son on narcotics charges. Apparently, he was selling but not using heroin. She complained bitterly about her son not getting any chances to succeed in society. Undereducated and black, where was he going to get anything better than some mickey-mouse, fast-food job.

Inadvertently, Colerain glanced over at the crying mother and their eyes met.

"Can I help you?" she commented sarcastically.

"No, but can I help you, you seem to be in distress?" Colerain replied.

"Asshole, mind your own business," she bellowed while glaring at him.

"Sure," he said. "I was just wondering what society might have done so wrong to your teenage son that he had to revert to being a drug dealer?"

"You aren't black, you can't understand." Her eyes narrowed as she spoke.

"Have you received assistance or help from our society during your life or during the raising of your son?" Colerain politely asked.

"I take whatever I can get from this uncaring, racist society. They owe it to me for all of the past injustices," she responded with earnest passion.

"Good luck with your son," he said while peering into her alert brown eyes.

She shook her head and waved him off with her right hand while returning her attention to her lunchmate. Sardonically, she commented, "That fool doesn't understand anything."

Colerain felt compelled to add, "With all of the help and assistance that you probably received from this sometimes racist society, the least you could have given back to this country is a good citizen."

The woman, this time, mildly replied, "Fuck you," then returned her focus toward her salad.

Chapter 34

"A BRIEF ENCOUNTER"

Colerain was never impressed with his wealth. He spent modestly, donated to chosen causes, and gave generously to those who provided him good service. He thought it unwise to excessively display his wealth. He realized that promoting the bounty of his inheritance would draw him unwanted attention and possibly foster envy. He knew that humans could become uncivilized over money. He realized the need for the future disbursement of his sizable assets and had a legal will and last testament provisions documented.

He had just exited a Pennsylvania State Store after purchasing two bottles of Santa Marita rose and a bottle of Soltero tequila. In the Keystone State, the only way to purchase wine or spirits was from these state-controlled liquor stores. You could not legally purchase those products in a grocery or convenience store as you could in the other forty-eight states. (Utah is the other exception.) Colerain, like many Pennsylvania residents, thought the system archaic and that it deserved to be eliminated.

While walking toward his parked vehicle, he encountered a man and his son. The child appeared to be about three years old. As they approached each other, Colerain offered a pleasant, "Good morning."

The young black father replied, “Good morning.”

The little boy then asked his father, “Who is that, Daddy?”

His daddy answered, “Just a nice man.”

The brief encounter provided Colerain with a pleasant thought. “I am a nice man.”

Chapter 35

"LEFT IN HIS HEAD"

Colerain has now been able to remove all thoughts of three women from his head. With Anye joining Erica and Jodie in death, he had envisioned some relief from the constant and consuming thoughts of his failed and painful relationships.

While he was in Gina's company or with friends, he was free from the burdens of thought that weighed so heavily upon him. When he worked, read, or created, he was free. When he entertained or was being entertained, the thoughts were not present to confound or trouble him. Other times, and what seemed like every waking moment, thoughts of another woman flourished. He desperately sought relief. The three others had been eliminated and now, this fourth woman and the thoughts of her needed to depart and join his other tormentors.

Most humans, men and women, probably have occasional thoughts about a lost or rejected love. The vast majority of people seem to be able to accept the loss and deal with the occasional ache of missing someone. Those who continue to love or possibly worship someone after rejection, separation, or even death are probably good candidates for intervention or counseling.

Colerain, sometimes, pondered whether to seek counsel or intervention. Did he feel guilt at any time for taking the lives of three perfectly good human beings? No, no, and no were his responses when he thought of those questions.

With no timetable in mind, he began to set into motion the planning for a final cleansing. Tiumes had rejected him most coldly and without warning. She was a collector of men. She loved them, used them, and when she grew tired or unfulfilled by them, she simply discarded her lovers. No discussion and no reason was ever offered or provided.

Tiumes (pronounced tee-u-mays) Maggic was now thirty-four years old and twenty-five years younger than Colerain. Her mother was a Cambodian refugee who found sanctuary in America during the late 1960s. She met her future Irish-American husband at Fort Indiantown Gap, Pennsylvania, where she was being processed along with thousands of other Southeast Asian immigrants.

Evann Maggic was an army officer and desk jockey who coordinated the paperwork of the health examinations and evaluations given to the refugees by a U.S. Army medical team. Evann was struck by the beauty of Leng Tygans and her ability to converse in English. Like many other Southeast Asian refugee women, the bright young woman saw this caring, handsome American as a possible vehicle to remove her from her current strife-filled and miserable circumstances that she was enduring. She sensed that she might find love, safety, and a home. Besides, this country had so much to offer if she could find a prosperous and loving American to marry. She envisioned herself living a life without fears and worries.

Their marriage produced one child, Tiumes, born in 1978. Evann Maggic loved and provided for his wife and daughter during their three years together. He was kind, considerate, and financially provided for all of their material needs. Because of Leng's diminutive physical stature and her almost total lack of breasts, he was rarely physically attracted to her. He loved her dearly, but he sought others to satisfy his sexual needs. Always carrying along some guilt, he meandered among several available women until he focused upon a busty Greek-American who enticed him to abandon his family. In 1981 Leng and Evann divorced. Leng obtained full custody of their three-year-old daughter and Evann religiously made monthly child support payments for the next fifteen years, never missing a monthly obligation. The amount eventually reached $580.00 per month during her teenage years.

Evann spent very little time with his daughter, Tiumes. Mother and daughter had relocated to central Pennsylvania and resided in Clover, a bustling suburb of Harrisburg. Leng was able to educate herself and was trained and earned a license as a life insurance agent for a national company.

Tiumes was a bright and clever child, yet average by school standards, and had many friends. By her high school years, she had developed into an attractive Amerasian beauty that many boys hovered around, constantly seeking her attention. Known to her classmates as the "Oriental hot-box," she surrendered her virginity to a varsity high school basketball player when she was fifteen.

Her father received an occasional photograph of his daughter, along with some current lifetime information about her, but he unilaterally elected not to pursue any involvement in her life. When Tiumes turned eighteen, support payments ceased and Evann Maggic concentrated his total attention toward his wife, their four children, and a pair of beagle hounds. Economically, life finally improved for the Maggic family.

Tiumes might have been referred to as a latchkey child, and by age ten, she was preparing staple and nutritious meals for her mother and herself besides taking responsibility for maintaining the cleanliness of their home. Leng's successful insurance career required extended workdays and commitments that did allow her to provide her daughter a comfortable home and most of her material wants and needs. Tiumes was gifted academically, yet she regularly earned only C+ or B- grades throughout her elementary and secondary schooling. Something, obviously, is to be stated about parental involvement during a child's educational and social development. Too often, Tiumes was left to her own directional compass when it came to meaningful progress in those areas.

She entered a state teachers college after her graduation from high school. The college was about two hours' drive from her home, a distance of some one hundred and twenty-five miles. Far enough away to savor independence, yet close enough to visit home when necessary. Usually, any high school graduate could gain admission to any of the colleges in the state system. A important aspect of America's great plan to provide college educational opportunities for the masses and, of course, to generate income for state and federal institutions.

Going to college became the ultimate enjoyable experience for Tiumes. She partied, went to endless social activities and sporting events, and relished the unbroken projection of unbridled freedom. Her earned grades were average, mostly Cs, with her GPA hovering slightly above 2.0. She pursued her courses with irregular effort, seldom exerting the required energy to ensure success in her studies and research.

Tiumes recognized herself as an exotic, attractive young woman, which prompted her to flirt constantly with males from all backgrounds and races. She delighted in shocking others with her conquests, pursuits, and fleeting relationships.

She often commented to friends, "I know that someday in America, all of the people will have the same caramel-colored skins. I'm a blender, Can't you tell?"

During her junior year she experienced an epiphany, or intuitive understanding, of an area of educational interest. She decided to become an education major with the intent of becoming a high school English or literature teacher. She began to study, read, and write with a newfound intensity and passion. Her assignments were taken seriously and it was easy to observe her progress represented by the regular A grades attained in her education courses.

At this stage of her life, most of her consistent friendships were with males, including a number of gays who had been able to become open about their sexuality. She dated and enjoyed the company of several young men. Sometimes she was criticized by others for appearing to be nothing but a collector of men, someone who tried to get as many men interested in her as possible, providing no intention of ever getting serious with any of her conquests. She wasn't a whore in any sense of that word. She surrendered her pleasures to a select few while primarily teasing and tempting others to extended periods of distraction.

After completing student teaching requirements, she graduated with a Bachelor of Arts degree in education, then earning teacher certification by passing a battery of rigorous state-mandated examinations. She was qualified to teach English for grades seven through twelve in the public and private schools of her home state. She believed that she could become an effective teacher and teenage motivator.

Both her student-teaching cooperating teacher and her college supervisor wrote glowing recommendations for Tiumes as she diligently pursued a beginning to her career in education.

Chapter 36

"SEEING BEFORE THE HEARING"

In late January 2002 Colerain Pike was summoned, via registered mail, to attend a hearing at the central administration offices of his part-time employer, the local board of education. He had witnessed an alleged drug transaction in a stairwell at a high school where he was addressing some members of the faculty on the merits of investing in 401 and 403B retirement plans. He signed in at the main entrance security desk, after producing photographic identification and proof of valid employment. He proceeded to walk soundlessly through the arch of a metal detector assuring the vigilant female monitor that he was "clean" to enter the facility.

Colerain usually declined to ride elevators, preferring the cardio charge he received by walking up interior staircases. His heart rate increased as he exited the stairwell into the fourth floor corridor while searched for room 458, Human Resources. The door to the office dated to the construction timeframe of this administration building. A mid-1920s structure built to portray the importance of the facility. Featured extensively throughout the building were stone walls, hardwood flooring, wrought iron railings, and a noticeable number of stained glass windows.

The door to Human Resources was a massive, walnut-stained barrier with an opaque and pebbled glass insert that shifted slightly when the door opened and closed. Colerain considered reaching out to steady the three-by-five-foot sheet of silicate and sand, but he drew back, thinking that a few lines of caulking would someday be inserted.

The front desk secretary commanded an unobstructed view of the entrance portal from her sparsely decorated and featureless desk. If a person could be described as birdlike, the forty-six-year-old Debra Novelle would easily fit that description. Her lean and willowy stature, with straight chin-length blonde hair and piercing ice-blue eyes, gave the secretary an appearance of a hawk-like predator.

"Mr. Pike, I presume," she cawed. "Dr. Bozaniak and the hearing officer are expecting you. I'll buzz them to inform them of your timely arrival."

"Thank you, Ms. Novelle," Colerain replied, noting her name on her desk's nameplate.

"Ms. Maggic?" the secretary inquired of the young woman seated to her right who was intently reviewing a packet information detailing possible employment.

"Yes, Miss," she answered.

"Dr. Bozaniak should be able to speak to you shortly in reference to your application for substitute teaching after this hearing. I hope that you will tolerate any delays. You must realize that Dr. Bozaniak is a very busy and important man," she lectured.

"No problem, I have some paperwork to complete while I wait," she replied.

"You just do that, young lady," the hawk-like predator droned sarcastically.

Tiumes Maggic was twenty-four, attractive, and professionally dressed in a dark blue micro pinstripe women's business suit. She wore stylishly pointed three-inch heels that allowed her suit pants to hang perfectly, barely an inch above the carpeted office floor. Her dark brown hair was recently salon cut and tastefully nipping at her shoulders. She didn't appear to have pupils in her extremely dark brown, slightly almond-shaped eyes. Carmine-colored lipstick appeared to be the only makeup that she applied, which contrasted against her brilliantly white teeth. Her modest bodice indicated rather small breasts. Colerain referred to small breasts as petite tetons, and he thought that exactly as he looked toward the young woman.

Ms. Maggic glanced at Colerain and their eyes met momentarily. She smiled demurely and her tanned cheeks began to evolve into a slightly blushing tone of pink. At that moment, Colerain realized that her face contained some Asian features. He noted that her nose was a little wider and slightly blunter than most Caucasian noses. Her almond-shaped eyes had very short eyelashes, usually common in many Asian people. Was she partly of Philippine descent? He couldn't be sure. He believed that she was definitely a combination of European and Asian blending, Colerain felt emotionless in regards to the drug transaction hearing that he was to undergo. Yes, he had witnessed the drug sale. A young black male, a fifteen-year-old sophomore from Springtown, was selling four ounces of marijuana to three sixteen-year-old females from the upper-class neighborhood of Coventry Hill. The girls appeared to be elated buying the weed from the young dealer, seemingly thrilled to be making their purchase in the south stairwell of their school. The $100.00 worth of cannabis sativa was meant for some partying during the upcoming weekend and was a regular feature of their social scene. Drug dealing was so pervasive on the school grounds that safeguards to preventing the activity were frequently ignored.

Colerain happened to walk into the stairwell precisely as money and the marijuana were changing hands. Chole Spiker, Amanda Klein, Briana Hirsch, and Andre Tate all froze.

The now frozen students could have bolted and ran. The purchase had just been witnessed by an adult. Besides, all activity in the school, in all areas, including stairwells, were under continuous video surveillance. They were busted.

Tiumes Maggic spoke to Colerain. "In a bit of trouble, are you, Mr. Pike?"

"Yes," he replied. "Unfortunately, I walked into the middle of a drug deal that involved what appeared to be four decent kids. I don't know if these students are bold, stupid, or simply careless. Apparently, the atmosphere in some schools too often signals that they are Freedom High. You can basically do what you want with little or no consequences."

"Well, good luck in the hearing," she added.

"Thanks," Colerain replied..

The phone of the hawk predator rang once. Ms. Novelle picked up, listened intently, and then informed Colerain that the hearing was about to commence.

He rose from his seat, smoothed out the front of his slacks, and walked toward Tiumes Maggic. He extended his hand, and while shaking hands he stated, “It was very pleasant speaking to you, Ms. Maggic. Good luck in obtaining some employment. I’m sure that your efforts will be rewarded.”

She smiled and thanked Colerain and added, “It was very nice meeting you, Mr. Pike.”

Chapter 37

"HEARING"

The red dot blinking on his answering machine indicated six new or recent telephone messages. Four were from the same phone number, all from his investment specialist superior, one from a telephone number that Colerain didn't recognize, and one from the school district.

He checked a woman's message first. The caller shared brief thoughts indicating her desires, suggestions, and innuendos. Colerain was enticed by this unexpected message.

His investment superior, Milton Rawsky, reminded Colerain of a dinner meeting to update his ever-expanding portfolio on Thursday at Trugats Middle Eastern restaurant scheduled for 7:00 p.m.

The final message was from the hawk-like Ms. Novelle. He was instructed to return to the Education Central Administration Building, room 209, 7:30 a.m. this coming Wednesday. Also, he was reminded that this hearing concerned the drug transaction that he "allegedly" witnessed in a drug-free school zone.

The first, initially unrecognized and nameless, yielded a message from Ms. Tiumes Maggic. In a sweet and slightly raspy voice she indicated her pleasure in meeting Colerain and suggested that they meet in the near future for some coffee, iced tea, or a glass of Tanqueray and tonic. Colerain was puzzled how she might have known that his preferred choice of gin was Tanqueray. Smiling, he thought she might be a private investigator.

Chapter 38

"LACK OF JUSTICE"

Colerain drove into the education complex parking lot and was greeted by a young man wearing a Boyton security company uniform. The basic gray jacket and cargo pants were trimmed with red and black stripes at the cuffs and collar. A shoulder-mounted communication device, flashlight, and retractable baton were the only defensive or safety features of the uniform. The guard, Antonio Thompson, immediately recognized Colerain and waved him in without checking his ID or requiring a parking voucher. He recalled the polite conversation they had in the past week.

Colerain was pleased to see Antonio and appreciated the special treatment and recognition that the guard provided, As was his nature, he tipped the attendant handsomely and was directed to a prime parking spot near the administrative building's main entrance.

As expected, security at the entrance was extensive. All visitors needed to show a photo ID, indicate their purpose, have their name checked against a master admit list and make a clean pass through the metal detection doorway device. Colerain's entrance was expected and predictably uneventful.

He climbed one flight of stairs, stepped into the second-floor hallway, and immediately spied room 209. He entered the room at precisely 7:29 a.m. Four secretaries or office personnel were seated at their desks behind a long four-foot-high wooden counter that was covered with a thick glass top. The four secretaries, all women and African American, were in their fifties and dressed stylishly, as if there was some dressing competition with one another.

One woman, glaring intently, barked at Colerain. "Mr. Pike, you're late. Everyone else had arrived minutes ago. You are expected in conference room B." As he approached the conference room door, the secretary turned toward her office colleagues and announced, "Another black kid getting railroaded."

Colerain took a quick notice of her desk name plate. Ramona Robinson, he may need that information at some future crossing.

Upon entering the conference room, he was immediately aware of the large number of individuals seated around the long rectangular table. At the head of the table sat the hearing officer; next to her, on her right, was an empty seat which she gestured to Colerain to occupy.

As Colerain was taking his seat, he completed a rapid count of the twenty people already in position around the massive blacktopped table. He recognized the four students: Andre Tate, Chole Spiker, Amanda Klein, and Briana Hirsch. He listened as the hearing officer introduced herself to the gathering as Mrs. Flora Nayarit.

Mrs. Nayarit was forty-ish, short in stature, and dressed in a sienna brown-colored business skirt suit with a plain, long-sleeved white blouse. She glanced at her gold-toned wristwatch and in a clear and authoritative voice, she stated that the hearing was about to commence and that she expected acceptable conduct and decorum throughout the proceedings.

Without prepared notes, Mrs. Nayarit indicated that she would introduce all of the individuals in attendance starting at her left. "This is Officer Wadsworth, from the school district police. He will remove any person who disrupts any part of these proceedings. Next to him is Amanda Klein, then her parents, Dr. and Mrs. Isaac Klein. Seated next to Mrs. Klein is Mr. Abe Brewster, their family attorney. Next is Mr. and Mrs. David Spiker and their daughter Chole. Mr. Spiker, you are an attorney, I presume?"

"Yes, madam," he replied.

She continued, "To Chole's left we have Dr. Noah Hirsch, Briana, and two attorneys representing the family, Ms. Rachel Yost and Mr. Solomon Durkin. Seated next to Mr. Durkin is Ms. Janet Hallern, esteemed school board member, representing the fifth district. Next to Ms. Hallern we have Ms. Kiesha Tolliver, Andre Tate's mother;

Mrs. Carole Tolliver, Andre's grandmother; and Andre. To Andre's left is Mr. Kendrell Parker, Andre's uncle; Mr. Mojave Gaston, who is Andre's stepbrother; and finally Ms. Kellie Coleman, Andre's sister. And next to me is Mr. Colerain Pike, visitor and financial advisor."

"There better be no railroadin' of my brother. He did nothing wrong. This trial better be fair, I know that the boy is innocent," Ms. Coleman abruptly commented.

"Officer Wadsworth, escort Ms. Coleman to the visitors' waiting area. If she doesn't cooperate, she can be cuffed and transferred to the Level District Police Station," Mrs. Nayarit ordered.

The police officer rose and walked around to Ms. Coleman. Without offering any protest, she stood and allowed herself to be escorted from the conference room.

All of the other hearing participants watched silently as this indication of control from Mrs. Nayarit unfolded. Colerain thought, as might others, that it would be obvious who would conduct and control these proceedings.

Mrs. Flora Nayarit cleared her throat and read the following statement: "In violation of school code B-14, these four students were observed by an adult visitor and video surveillance participating in an illegal drug transaction on school district property."

At least a half-dozen voices rang out at the completion of her statement. Mrs. Nayarit raised her voice and her right hand simultaneously. "All individuals involved in this hearing will speak only when they are called upon or recognized. Is that understood?" she said while glaring at the occupants of the table.

A few faint murmurs of yes could be heard coming from the gathering.

Officer Wadsworth reentered the conference carrying a business-size white envelope, which he handed to the hearing officer. She removed the single sheet of plain unlined paper and unfolded it. As she read its contents, her stern yet attractive face instantaneously turned a bright shade of crimson.

"Who gave this to you, Officer?" she inquired.

He answered, "Police Chief Bojanski. He said to give it to you immediately."

Mrs. Nayarit cleared her throat, wiped her brow with her left hand, and announced, "All charges were being dropped against the four high school students. Apparently, the four-ounce bag of marijuana that was confiscated has been lost and cannot therefore be used as evidence. This hearing has ended. You are all free to go.

Students, report back to school as soon as you can this morning. And, consider yourselves very, very fortunate."

Everyone quickly departed from the conference chamber except Mrs. Nayarit and Mr. Colerain Pike.

"I can't believe this," Colerain said aloud.

Flora countered, "It's bullshit. The chief or some school board member must have been pressured or persuaded to recommend this abortion of justice. Did you see all of the damn lawyers? How about the entourage for Andre Tate?" she continued.

"I guess the administrators and teachers in our schools need to act like those three monkeys who see, speak, and hear nothing. Good day, Mrs. Nayarit," Colerain commented as he stood to leave.

"Be safe, and thanks," answered Flora Nayarit.

Chapter 39

"A LITTLE TELECOMMUNICATION"

Colerain spent about twenty-five minutes at the aborted meeting. It was barely 8:00 a.m. when he exited the administration building. While walking, he took his newly acquired cell phone and hit the redial button for the saved telephone number of Tiumes Maggic. On the third ring she picked up.

Her early morning, raspy voice (unusual, yet alluring, he thought) answered, "Hello, Cole-rayne," extending the last syllable.

"Hey there," Colerain replied. "I received your message. I have some time off today. and I thought that you might be available to step out for some breakfast."

"I'd love to," she began. "But why don't you come to my place for some blackberry flapjacks and some Argentinian coffee that I was just about to percolate."

"I wouldn't want to impose upon you, Ms. Maggic. Besides, I should have thought that you are probably getting ready to get to work," he countered.

She said, "Call me Tiumes, and no work for me today. Look, my house is at 1141 Rosedale Road over in Cypress Park. Fourth house on the right with a maroon-colored canvass awning covering my front porch. Please join me, Colerain."

How could he refuse breakfast with this beautiful and exotic woman who did a fabulous job of initiating this encounter. She is about fifteen minutes away in that splendid Cypress Park area, he thought.

"I will see you in about a half hour, Tiumes," he responded.

"Great, see ya," Tiumes said as she hung up her phone.

Chapter 40

"BLACKBERRIES FLOWING OVER, AND THEN SOME"

The house on 1141 Rosedale was a dark, red-brick two-story. Colerain thought it was a pleasant-looking structure. Newer, white-trimmed windows with colonial muntins provided a breath of contrast to the dark brick and dark-colored tile roof. The front porch had a two-seat wooden swing suspended from the porch ceiling, and the maroon awning provided almost complete privacy with its extended sloping form. Scanning the porch, he noticed a ceramic lizard climbing upon some loose stones in a bowl that was placed to the right of the woven rattan welcome mat. He pushed the bell button of a brassy goldfish and waited.

Tiumes appeared at the entrance within seconds, pushing open the screen door and quietly saying to Colerain, "Get in here, you."

She was wearing what appeared to be some type of kimono. It was floor length with three-quarter-length sleeves and was attractively decorated with embroidered flowers and representations of wading birds. The kimono front was secured by eight light green-colored buttons that represented dragonflies. On her feet were a pair of bright white socks.

"Are you hungry?" she asked, as she released a glowing gaze upon her visitor.

"I could eat a little," he replied.

Tiumes noted Colerain's attire. A dark navy blue tailored suit bearing tiny, light blue pinstripes. His slacks were cuffed, barely covering his expensive Italian leather dress shoes. His brilliantly white, long-sleeved shirt was enhanced by a scarlet-colored silk tie that was decorated by minute white diamond shapes. She detected no jewelry except for the modest outline of a gold chain peeking out near the top of his shirt collar. She thought that he looked amazingly handsome.

In what was unusual for a house, the room they entered after walking through the front doorway was the kitchen.

"I call this the first kitchen," she explained. "Much of a home's living takes place in the kitchen. That is why I chose to locate mine at the front door. Besides, I can keep my place much cleaner and tidier."

"I never thought of it, but it's a great idea and it's a wonderfully designed use of space," he answered truthfully. "This is a very engaging room," he added.

An island of black stone marble was set proudly as the center stage in the spacious environment. A ceramic tray, oval in shape, held a carafe of coffee, two handmade pedestal ceramic mugs, one spoon, and a glass bowl overflowing with a bounty of blackberries. Tiumes selected one plump berry, allowing a few others to tumble from the bowl onto the countertop. She lifted the fruit to his lips as he opened them ever so slightly.

"Mmmm, delicious," was his reaction.

"I picked a quart of these babies this morning from a patch of blackberries in the wooded area behind my backyard," she beamed.

Colerain reached into the glass bowl and selected an especially dark and swollen berry. He raised it to Tiumes' lips and gently rubbed the fruit along the outline of her mouth. He stopped in the center of her upper lip, at the cupid's bow, then along her philtrum to the tip of her slightly flattened nose. Juices from the ripened berry were leaving a painted trail of sweetness along its outlined pathway.

He ceased decorating and casually placed the blackberry into his own mouth and savored the indulgence.

The distance between their faces was less than a foot. Colerain closed that space by 90 percent as he moved closely toward her. Any man who is an experienced lover should reduce the space between himself and a woman. Then allow her to determine when the final 10 percent will be traversed.

Instantaneously Tiumes closed that gap and began to kiss Colerain passionately. Colerain, relishing the hint of berry upon her lips, returned the kisses and drew her into a series of intense embraces.

No words were spoken. If one was listening, only the sounds of ravenous kissing and the sounds produced by clothing being removed could be heard. The top buttons of her kimono were unhooked and Tiumes stepped out of her garment. She was wearing a spaghetti strap camisole and a transparent light blue thong. Somehow her white footsie socks had already discarded. The hardened points of her rather small nipples were pushing for their freedom against the thin blue top.

Colerain's suit coat, dress shirt, tie, and shoes had already been sent to the polished hardwood floor. He stood before her in suit pants, black socks, and a white wife-beater T-shirt. His readiness was obviously apparent to Tiumes as she took a quick downward glance.

He paused momentarily, turned, then lifted the ceramic tray and its contents and placed it upon the top of her nearby dishwasher. Colerain reached toward Tiumes and removed her top, then slid her thong down over her thighs, allowing her to step out of them. Her nakedness further stimulated this very visual man. Her breasts, small but firm, flawless legs, and perfect derriere were complemented by the Brazilian/bikini cut of her pubic hair.

Colerain lifted Tiumes and placed her into a sitting position atop the kitchen island. While his lips moved to devour her breasts, she removed the belt from his slacks. As they descended to the floor, she realized that he was commando and very energetically ready to have her way with him. Wearing only his wife-beater T-shirt, he scaled her island and presented himself for her and his enjoyment.

Chapter 41

"CELESTE RIVERS"

Colerain Pike was thirteen years old and looking forward to turning fourteen during that hot and humid summer thirty years ago. The daily high temperatures hovered around ninety, with humidity rates in the high eighties. Most homes lacked air-conditioning, including Colerain's. Living indoors and—worse yet—sleeping in a third-floor bedroom without a fan or ventilation was nearly impossible. During those summer days he hung out with friends, played basketball and tennis, and swam at his neighborhood's public swimming pool.

A great amount of attention and effort was paid to the young ladies of his neighborhood by Colerain and his friends. On a daily basis, he attempted to gain the favor of one pretty, sixteen-year-old girl. This young lady was about to begin her junior year in high school during the upcoming fall. Colerain would be entering ninth grade at the same facility.

Diane Taki had long, blonde, shoulder-length hair, which she parted precisely down the middle from the top of her head. Her eyes were blue and her sparkling white and perfectly straight teeth were displayed easily when she spoke or smiled. Colerain was most attracted to a feature that the majority of his peers agreed was Diane's best asset: She had rather large breasts.

Colerain intentionally looked for opportunities to speak with Diane. He would try to arrange for encounters where it might appear that he had simply and coincidentally walked into her. Diane never showed any indication of faint interest in talking to the younger teenager. Usually, she responded to any of his conversational attempts with complete disinterest or a sassy remark of dismissal.

Early one Saturday morning, as he was walking out of a local corner drugstore named Paddys, he accidentally walked directly into the path of the unseen Diane Taki. The young lady was momentarily knocked off of her stride.

She angrily blurted to the teenager, "You asshole, you almost ran me over."

Colerain had reached out, caught her, and prevented her from falling, but as he did he inadvertently touched her ample right breast.

She yelled, "You're just trying to feel me up."

"No, no, no," replied Colerain, "I didn't try to do that to you. I'm sorry"

"If you ever touch me again I'll get my cousin, Henry Talkovich, to kick your ass," she barked while staring at the embarrassed teenager. With a peculiar look upon her face and, clearly unexpectedly, she added, "I must admit though, that you are kinda cute."

After she regained her composure, she walked away while Colerain stared intently at her behind while slowly nodding his head in approval.

From an unknown location, he was startled by a woman's voice calling out to him. "Hey kid, would you go into Paddys and buy me a pack of Kent cigarettes?" She then allowed a single dollar bill to leave her hand. It fluttered downward toward him from her second-floor apartment window, above Milo's confectionery store.

The woman was thirtyish with dishwater blonde hair and in possession of a very attractive face. She was wearing a canary yellow terrycloth bathrobe and held the top of it together with her bright red-tipped fingers. Colerain speared the fluttering currency and indicated that he would make the purchase for her.

She added, "Bring the smokes and the change up to my apartment, number 201."

Colerain nodded and walked into the corner store to purchase the cigarettes. (There was no age limit for cigarette purchases.) He then walked back directly to the doorway leading to the second-floor apartments above Milos. The cost of the pack of cigarettes was thirty-seven cents. He pocketed the sixty-three cents in change. Taking the steps two at a time, he bounded up to the second-floor hallway. Number 201 was on his left, facing the street. He lightly knocked and Celeste Rivers quickly opened the unbolted door.

She said, "Don't just stand there, young man. Come in and close that door."

Somewhat surprised, Colerain did as he was directed.

The terrycloth bathrobe that Miss Rivers wore was less tightly pulled together, allowing the teen to take a peek at her cleavage. Celeste noticed that the teenager was staring rather than looking.

"May I have my change back, the sixty-three cents?" she requested. "I was going to give you a quarter for running that errand for me until I heard how rudely that little bitch was speaking to you. Now, I've decided to give you something better," she added. As she was speaking, she opened her bathrobe and revealed her breasts to him. Although stunned momentarily, he immediately began to feel a response rising below his waist.

Celeste requested that he move closer with a beckoning of her hands. Colerain moved closer. She pulled down his denim shorts and boxers then proceeded to thank him in a special way for completing the errand for her. The teenager felt truly blessed to have been provided this unexpected pleasurable experience.

During the weeks of that summer Celeste provided the young Colerain with many opportunities to explore and enjoy his blossoming sexuality. He gained valuable knowledge about sexual acts, their positions, and endless variables. Naively, he believed that Celeste Rivers was totally amazing and that they must be falling in love. Obviously, at almost fourteen. he was still totally lacking in sophistication to understand his complex "relationship."

Chapter 42

"PAIN IS WHAT THE PERSON EXPERIENCING PAIN SAYS IT IS"

Near the end of August, a week before his return to school, Celeste let Colerain know that she was planning on moving out of state and wanted to see him one more time before she departed. She suggested that he pay her a visit on a Friday afternoon, the day of her departure. Colerain, as usual, was excited and stimulated about the opportunity to visit Celeste. Realistically he knew that the favorable times with her were ending. He was preparing his feelings and emotions to be soothed and healed with the passing of time. Colerain always took the steps to her apartment by twos, opened her door, and entered without knocking.

Celeste turned to face him as he stepped into her sanctuary. With a scowl forming on her face, she spoke, "Can't you knock on the door, you little fuck?"

Her reaction startled Colerain as he replied, "I just thought . . ."

"All right, no big deal," she said "It's just a good idea to use some common courtesy sometimes."

Celeste knew that he wanted to have intercourse with her, but she had in her possession another plan.

"Colerain, my dear, I won't be able to let you have me because I'm on my damn period. You understand? But how about if I pose completely nude for you and you can take care of yourself. I'd love to see you do that. It would be a major turn-on for me," she quietly explained.

She removed her tank top, jean shorts, bra, and panties and sat upon her slightly worn, tan-colored couch. The teen became aroused immediately, and with some gentle prodding from Celeste, he pulled down his shorts and boxers. Within seconds his eyes closed while the image of Celeste burned into his memory. As he was nearing orgasm, Celeste provided oohing sounds of encouragement. As he began to explode, two, three, then four flashes of intensely bright lights radiated toward him.

He opened his eyes, and with his vision distorted by the flashes, he squinted to observe two male friends of Celeste's using flash cameras. Once again, two more bursts of intense light obscured his vision.

Colerain roared, "What the hell are you doing? Why are you taking my picture?" And finally, "Who are you?"

Celeste interrupted, "These are two of my friends who need some photographs for a men's magazine that they are putting together. Colerain, you just made yourself twenty dollars."

"I don't want their damn money. What kind of pervert do you think I am?" he bellowed as hot, salty tears streamed down the cheeks of his face. He then pulled up his shorts to cover his vulnerability. "I hate you, Celeste. Why did you allow this to happen? You planned this?" he cried, trembling with rage.

"Colerain, I make money, you make money, and these queens make money. Besides, don't worry, your name will never be used with these photos. Don't worry, this won't hurt you, I promise," she added.

Colerain drew nearer to the two photographers with clenched fists and spat at them. "I hate you, I'll hope you both die," he spewed.

The two men laughed and mocked him by rubbing their eyes and massaging their own genital areas.

"Go, Colerain, leave now," Celeste ordered quietly.

Chapter 43

"CERTAIN COLLATERAL DAMAGE"

Colerain ached. The severity and depth of his complex pain seemed impossible to alleviate. He was angry, devastated, humiliated, violated, embarrassed, and somehow, even disappointed and cheated.

Under the cover of night, he tossed a two-pound, red pavement brick through the window of Celeste's apartment. Shards of glass exploded from her apartment window, raining upon all nearby surfaces below. He ripped her mailbox from its moorings, hoping that a crepuscular feline would welcome the opportunity to urinate upon its scattered contents. He constantly thought of other ideas to deliver more certain damage to the perpetrators of his morally repulsive experience.

The morning following the window shattering, he was on the street drawn to the apartment of Celeste Rivers. Her vehicle was no longed parked in its customary spot; he assumed that she had departed. Inadvertently, he noticed one of the two photographers loading some equipment into the front trunk of a black Volkswagen beetle bearing an orange-colored New York state license plate. He stepped back into a doorway to avoid detection. He watched as the bearded young man closed the trunk and walked back toward the apartment entrance.

Impulsively Colerain sprinted one city block and into the entrance of the nearby Swartzmiller family supermarket. There were a few early-morning customers and a skeleton crew of employees scattered about the aisles of the store. He walked unnoticed into the aisle where condiments were stocked. He slipped a one-pound bag of granulated white sugar under his long T-shirt. Then he exited the store unnoticed.

A quickened pace brought him to the parked black VW bug. He opened the hood mounted gas cap and poured the contents of the bag of sugar into the fuel line of the vehicle. He brushed the sugar crystals from his hands and screwed the gas cap back in place. Believing he went unnoticed, he headed home. He considered his deed and savored the imminent ramifications of his actions.

Chapter 44

"GUILT AND TRYING TO UNDERSTAND"

Colerain was not able to maintain thoughts of hate, nor was he able to permanently despise the freelance photographers. In fact, he attempted to comprehend the life choices that the men appeared to embrace. Whether their sexuality was acquired, selected, or dictated to by a biological requirement, these men—and apparently hundreds of thousands of others—were gay. He did realize that they were involved in a form of commerce or business. And, even though naïve, he rationalized that when there is a market for a product, someone will fill that particular need. His experience may have resulted simply from commerce. He was exploited because he was made available.

After his initial shock and disappointment toward Celeste Rivers, his disgust toward her abated. She did place herself in a position to be a procurer for the two New Yorkers, but she may have believed that no harm would come to Colerain. She frequently seemed to need money, and with no marketable skills or specialized education, she saw only the financial reward of that specialized commerce. He remembered that he heard one of the men indicate to her that she earned $150 for her role in his painful summer evening.

Celeste provided the young Colerain with several sexual opportunities that he never believed that he was tricked or forced into. The evolution of his sexual experience did not follow the course commonly traveled by most young men in society. More often the young man must gain his woman's trust, present her with gifts to display his affection, cultivate their relationship, and then convince her to share with him her pristine sexuality. Teachers, ministers, employers, coaches, and others who use their position of power or influence to rob a young woman of her favors deserve to be punished to the fullest extent of the law. Probably some women in similar positions use the same techniques as men to harvest young males for similar gratification. Although Colerain did believe that he was exploited, truthfully he felt that he obtained the greatest benefits from his sexual encounters with Ms. Rivers.

She educated him about a man making love to a woman. She was the mentor who explained sensitivity, positioning, erotic zones, preferences, dislikes, and exploration during sexual activity. The teenager had experienced and learned so much from the thirty-two-year-old maven. Should he hate her?

He was able to relish the thoughts of his ability to extract an economic pound of flesh from the photographers. The New York duo's Volkswagen would suffer some severe engine damage, probably in its first twenty miles of travel. Repairs could easily cost between two and three hundred dollars. Celeste would lose most of her security deposit that she had paid when she signed a rental agreement. The window repair, mailbox replacement, and general clean-up fee would probably cost her half of her initial one-hundred-dollar apartment deposit.

Chapter 45

"FATES AND CIRCUMSTANCES"

Colerain realized from his experience that a woman and the powerful attraction of her sex could allow her to maintain almost complete control over a man. He would have done almost anything that Celeste would have asked or solicited him to do. He blamed the convulsive ending to his experience upon himself. He could not deny that he must always be the person that controls and takes full responsibility for his actions. He was able to accept the blame and shoulder the guilt for his life-altering mistake. Yet he knew some day that he might be able to look at these mistakes as nothing more than harmless peccadilloes.

In his fourteenth summer, the bright and attractive young man learned one of the most important lessons of his life. He knew that there would be a serious price to pay for any woman who used or manipulated Colerain Pike in any future relationships. Through his training with Celeste, he acquired skills, and he would use them, if necessary, to gain advantages over any woman or girl that he cultivated an interest in. Of course, it might be a challenge to maintain the cold and self-serving demeanor necessary for using those advantages if he would find himself caring about any woman.

Chapter 46

"FIVE MONTHS THAT ROARED"

Colerain placed a phone call to the director of personnel at the Taviston Board of Public Education. Belinda Washington (has anyone ever noticed that few Caucasian people, besides George and Martha, have the surname of Washington?) was thirty-five, gorgeous, well educated (master's degree at Dartmouth), African American, and has held her position of personnel director for three years. Occasionally, she would pull some job placement strings. She was responsible for 95 percent of all hiring within the school district. She loved C. Pike. On a number of occasions, she and Colerain had enjoyed a number of golden opportunities to relish each other privately. One of her favorite rendezvous was when, totally naked, they made love atop her mahogany desk, while her office lights blazed at 10:00 a.m. on a Wednesday morning last April.

She would honor any legitimate placement request from Colerain, only if he promised an opportunity for their secret romancing.

"Hello, Ms. Washington's office," answered Mildred Tarfog, the private secretary of the director of personnel.

"This is Mr. Pike, Millie. How are you and your husband Eugene?" he inquired.

"Just fine, Mr. Pike. When are you going to visit again?" she literally sang to him. "I just love that Vector pen and mechanical pencil set that you gave to me during your last visit with Belinda, I mean, Ms. Washington."

"It seems that I'm always so busy, Mildred, but the next time that I stop in, maybe we can get a chance to chat and I just might have picked up something nice for you during my travels," he answered.

He spoke with Belinda and asked her to consider helping a young teacher that he had met recently. She was certified to teach high school English and would be able to present admirable recommendations and impressive teaching exam test scores. Belinda informed Colerain that an English teacher at Stoneridge High was about to begin a maternity leave in three weeks. Based upon his request and the quality of the application that she was currently reading online, she thought that Tiumes Maggic would be a good fit for the position. Belinda indicated that she would recommend her to fill a full-time substitute position for the expected ninety-day maternity leave. Also, because she was part Asian-American, her selection would fit nicely into the district's minority hiring quota directive.

"Colerain," Ms. Washington sang, "I have to work this Saturday morning. Would you like to come in and assist me with some filing and housekeeping?"

"This Saturday, do you mean this coming Saturday? Maybe I can bring in some sinful pastry and my video camera," he teased.

"Mister, just bring yourself. We might not have time for those other things," she ordered.

"Okay, madam director. I'll be there. And, please, my dear, no underwear, we might not have time for the unessentials," he countered.

"Mr. Pike, I can't wait, I just may attack you when you appear at my door. I'll see you around ten."

Chapter 47

"NEWLY HIRED, JUST KNEW SOMEBODY"

Tiumes called Colerain that evening, revealing to him her good fortune at being hired as a permanent full-time substitute for the school year's second semester. She was energized, excited, and talkative. He reminded her that her credentials were at a high level, and that the school district would be remiss not to hire her and prevent her from flourishing for another employer. He would not permit himself to inform her of his intervention. He also knew that Belinda Washington would be entirely professional and not mention the influence of Mr. Colerain Pike.

Tiumes attempted to coax Colerain to Rosedale Street to celebrate with her over a bottle of imported Chianti from Italy. He indicated that he had made other plans that were unbreakable. Actually, he committed to playing some Texas hold'em poker with some friends. Some time ago, he adjusted his encounters with his woman to occasionally deny her the pleasure of his company. He realized that making her want him more would only increase passion and lovemaking might become even more intense. He revealed this strategy to his card-playing friends; most admitted that they would not have the resolve to follow his lofty guidelines.

Chapter 48

"PERCEPTIONS"

She was not drop-dead gorgeous. She probably was never considered or referred to as eye candy, but she was pretty. Pretty, in a blended and somewhat exotic way. Sometimes he thought that Tiumes' facial features had the ability to change. At times, she appeared more Asian and on other occasions, her European-ness was more evident. Colerain, in particular, loved looking at her from behind. From the waist down, he thought that her form was perfect.

When they were together Tiumes often initiated physical contact and lovemaking. Her probing kisses and touching instantly commanded his attention and responses. Other times, he was the aggressor and her responses were equally passionate. After they had been seeing each other for about two months, she told him that she was afraid of the power that his passion held over her. She sensed that she would always be powerless to resist his advances. Colerain teased her and reminded her that women were the real power brokers in relationships. Tiumes always wanted Colerain to come to her house. She was not willing to share him with anyone else. He appreciated that posture, but he also knew that he could exit her circle occasionally into another direction if he desired. For the most part, her possessiveness was acceptable to him.

Tiumes was seldom comfortable enough to allow herself to be totally nude in front of Colerain. She would not allow him to sketch or draw her completely unclothed. Often, she would be naked from the waist down, proudly displaying those features. He could recall, and his memory was outstanding, only seeing her naked from the waist up on one occasion. She may have been uncomfortable exposing her breasts and nipples because they were decidedly small.

With the lights dimmed, and during lovemaking, her petite tetons were always actively involved. Nevertheless, she would never sit or walk around topless.

On one occasion, Tiumes expressed some concern about a mole on her right shoulder that she thought was changing and asked Colerain to look at it for her. He related to her that on his most recent visit to his dermatologist, the physician mapped all of his moles and photographed every region of his body for future reference. Tiumes asked him to map out and check all of her moles, but she would never feel comfortable being photographed. With a serious, and conscientious effort, he tried to search her dozens of moles. He admitted to being able to recognize a change to any blemish if it was very obvious. For the second time in Colerain's presence, she removed her top and appeared not be concerned about her nudity.

Her breasts were very small, with only a slight indication of weight to allow for any amount of volume.

He found that heavy, ponderous breasts were unattractive and even considered them to be sloppy, too often sliding around, falling by their weight to the woman's sides, or hanging or moving in an unappealing manner. When Tiumes realized that she had exposed her top to him, she became noticeably uncomfortable and immediately covered herself. Colerain wanted to approach her about the subject, but the timing was not appropriate.

After the mole mapping, he joked with her about seeing a copy of the Big Dipper in the middle of her back. She appeared to have become distant, yet they made love with her positioned on top. These revelations did not diminish, in any way, his interest in Tiumes. In fact, he was beginning to recognize the feelings that he had for her were becoming more advanced and complicated.

Chapter 49

"RIPPLES"

During the next four months the couple had many opportunities to spend time with each other. On most of those occasions, she preferred that he visit her at 1141 Rosedale Street. They rarely went out together publicly; when they did, it was to a nondescript bar or restaurant. He believed that Tiumes desired to have him solely to herself or possibly that she may have been unsure of herself dating a man twice her age. Their relationship remained serenely private.

On a few occasions, when Colerain teased or flirted innocently with another woman, he detected a spark of jealousy emanating from Tiumes. He never minded those sparks; he was perfectly satisfied with his focus upon her and when she displayed a little jealousy, he took it as a compliment. He realized that she had gotten into his head. He would admit that in conversation by reminding her that she had burrowed herself in there deeply. Meanwhile, within the secretive recesses of her brain, Tiumes began to view Colerain Pike as just another man gathered to complement her collection.

An investment client, Ria Rangeview, had shown considerable interest in Colerain. In passing, or during a guarded moment, she would offer him a comment or suggestive gesture that he interpreted as a plausible sign of interest. He had suspected that her husband,

Miguel, was gay. He believed that he possessed a sense, or type of gaydar, that allowed him to recognize if a particular man was homosexual. More often than not, he was correct. Besides, he once witnessed Miguel holding hands with and then kissing another man before entering a taxicab. That oboe player for the Metropolitan Symphony was a low-down brother and a player in the gay community. As noted previously, Colerain's visual memory of events was superb.

Once, unexpectedly, while socializing, at a popular martini bar, he spotted Ria and her gaze froze Colerain. Miguel was involved in an animated discussion with an attractive young musician with whom he had previously played music. Ria visited with Colerain. She informed him that she was extremely lonely because her husband seldom spent any meaningful time with her. He was always practicing, writing scores for music, or out with his friends.

She revealed to Colerain that she and her husband haven't had a sexual encounter in months. His excuse was his overwhelming fatigue, or that he was under tremendous pressure to maintain his high level of skill in his oboe playing. She told Colerain about wearing provocative outfits, or trying to come on to him totally naked, only to be dismissed. She questioned herself and tried new approaches, but generally he had no reaction and simply offered the same excuses.

She paused then stepped closer to Colerain and asked in a low, sultry voice, "Would you like to see me naked? What if I dripped some golden honey upon my myself? What would you do?"

He answered, "Ria, you are a very attractive woman, I doubt that I would be able to muster the strength or willpower to resist you."

Ria responded, "Do you think that we could meet without Miguel finding out?"

Colerain answered by saying, "Currently I am seeing another younger woman."

Ria said, "Don't you realize that younger women just use older, wealthier men and dump them when they get tired of them? No future in that for them."

Pausing, he replied, hoping to conceal his emotional reaction to her comment, "If she was to put me out with the trash or not, I would relish an opportunity to get to know you more intimately."

Chapter 50

"COLLECTOR"

Tiumes worked diligently to develop a relationship with her selected man. In addition to beauty and intelligence, she used guile and her particular talents for persuasion to obtain or collect desirable men. Usually, she was very challenging for a man to defend against. When she set her sights upon a certain man, she accepted the invitation to get him under her spell, enjoy his talents, and then add him to her collection. After acquiring a man, she quickly lost interest; then, casually, and with dignity, she decided when it was time to send him away.

When any man began to offer her expensive gifts, suggested meeting his family, or announced his love for her, those behaviors prompted an immediate turnoff. When Colerain indicated that she was in his head, her reaction proved to be no different. In reality, in a perverse way, she may have desired a man who was hard-edged, possibly bordering on abusive, whom she could never really be sure of his intentions.

Colerain was different than most of her additions. He was somewhat mysterious and a more complex man who would tease and occasionally deny her his favors. Other times, he displayed his physical power when he decided to control all aspects of their lovemaking. Too often, she thought, he spoke too highly of the attributes of other women that they knew. That behavior irritated her. Sadly, within herself, she felt it was possible that he realized that she had a negative fixation and unyielding disappointment about her own human form. He never made a reference or issue to her about that, but she knew that he read her thoughts exactly on that subject.

The day that Tiumes stopped seeing him, she refused his request to visit, stating that she didn't feel well and she was going to stay in bed with her aches and pains. She indicated that she would call him the next morning. That evening Colerain and a friend visited Sid Blacks, a Center City club. They ordered drinks. Colerain a Yuengling draft and his friend, a bottle of Champlain pilsner. He turned from his seat to survey the surroundings and immediately spotted Tiumes and three of her girlfriends. She caught his gaze and her face turned a brownish red.

He approached her and commented, "I see that you are feeling better."

She answered, "I'm so sorry, Colerain, it's the first time that I ever lied to you. Don't hate me."

He looked directly into her eyes and replied, "Enjoy your evening with your buds, Tiumes."

Tiumes walked back to the company of her friends without offering any reply.

Colerain's companion inquired, "Who was that Jewish girl?"

Colerain said, "Somebody's daughter that I know."

At 3:00 a.m. he received a voice message from Tiumes. Without listening to the voicemail, he pressed the delete button on his telephone answering machine.

Chapter 51

"REMAINING"

Tiumes was in Colerain's head. He had invited her in and allowed her to remain and to develop roots. He was not able to dismiss her emotionally or to expunge the exotic young woman. The powerful sense of rejection that was eroding his spirit could not be eliminated. He despised, with great passion, the knowledge that he was used and had ultimately been discarded. To his own discredit, he thought, he permitted himself to become just another man in the women's collection.

Colerain truly enjoyed his relationship with Gina, but he did not love her. Gina savored their relationship also, yet she offered no love, no heartfelt feelings for her man. Comfort, caring, pleasure, and an addiction to their lovemaking were more than satisfactory reasons to maintain their connection.

Gina and he would occasionally spend time with another interest. They both agreed that an arrangement of that nature might increase the passion and flavor for their own particular desires. Colerain met infrequently with Ria or Belinda, and Gina spent some time with a married Redtower superior who protected and enhanced her standing and status within the company. Life appeared to be going quite well for Gina and Colerain. They were comfortable and very satisfied with the parameters of their significant friendship.

Mr. Pike understood that the time was near at hand when he would be compelled to formulate a plan to eliminate the collector. The relentless festering within his head required treatment. He could not allow himself to be a trophy or collectable for any woman. In particular, Ms. Tiumes Maggic.

Chapter 52

"HOMETOWN"

Taviston, Pennsylvania, with a population of slightly over one hundred thousand residents, was located about fifty miles southeast of Pittsburgh. The city was one of the ten largest in Pennsylvania, similar in size to the cities of Erie or Reading. Because of its proximity to Pittsburgh, a sizeable segment of its population was employed in and around that metropolis. An efficient interstate highway system delivered the Taviston residents to their places of employment in an hour-long commute.

Taviston had three major employers: a Honda auto parts manufacturing center; the Amaranth Brewery, producers of a half-dozen national brands of beer; and a railroad car processing and refinement complex. Thousands of local citizens were employed by these three local giants. Salaries, health benefits, and incentives were emphasized and enjoyed by management and working-class employees alike. Most nationally known chains, name brand stores, and restaurants also offered positions of employment to any interested or capable resident. The unemployment rate for Taviston seldom rose above 2 percent and the city had earned a well-deserved reputation as a middle-class mecca. The cost of living, reasonable housing prices, and affordable property and business tax levels had created a desirable location to live and raise a family.

The population of Taviston was well represented by most of America's ethnic, racial, and religious groups. The city population was approximately 20 percent Hispanic, 15 percent African American, 10 percent from various Asian groups, and 55 percent Caucasian. The city of Taviston appeared to be one of America's better integrated cities. Education was valued and supported by all of the various groups. The school system boasted of its less than 5 percent high school dropout rate. Most families were nuclear with two employed parents. Most homeowners emphasized the benefits of a sound education.

Crimes rates were noticeably lower than national averages in all published categories. The city did have crime and vice, yet the totals were almost always modest, possibly because the need to commit crimes were lowered by the fruits of regular employment. The police force had 175 officers who were expected to be fair, courteous, and professional in servicing all of Taviston's citizens.

Sadly, during the past six months the city had experienced an unheard-of spike in the number of murders committed. Six murders was an alarming total and a cause for civic and law enforcement concern. The average number of homicides for the past five years had been four. The police department had earned a clearance rate of 95 percent, with one unsolved killing during those years. A ten-year-old fourth-grade girl had been kidnapped from the bedroom of her home, and the Amber alert was posted during the six days that she was missing. Divers found her remains while dredging a manmade lake located in a state park just south of the city. Her body had been weighed down with pavement bricks stuffed into her clothing. Her natural father was suspected as the prime suspect based upon a fiercely contested divorce and overlapping child custody disputes.

The afternoon that the child's remains were recovered and definitively identified, her father, along with a female passenger, apparently drove his SUV into a bridge abutment traveling at a speed of approximately ninety miles per hour. Most law enforcement investigators and the public believed that he committed suicide and murder by automobile. Crime scene investigators did determine that the brakes of the car failed to function. Because of their lack of certainty, the police continued to list the girl's murder and the death of her father and the estranged woman as incompletely solved.

The ability to clear major crimes, such as murders, always earned public praise until the capital crimes of the past half year. Three of the six other murders went unsolved. Those three appeared to have been committed by the same person, most likely a man who was suspected of being a member of the Taviston community. Constant pressure from political and civic leaders was applied on a regular basis upon law enforcement to arrest the perpetrator of those apparently linked homicides. The police department offered guidelines for safe and precautionary measures to be taken when traveling, socializing and home security suggestions. Police requested that the public report all instances of unusual or suspicious behaviors whenever they were observed. Of course, the police received hundreds of these alerts and promptly investigated them thoroughly. Most observations were easily explained and eliminated. Some were accusations aimed at certain men as a form of revenge by vengeful women who believed that they had been wronged or disrespected by a lover or suitor.

No new information was obtained during this period of time to provide the police with anything to assist them in their continuing investigation of the unsolved murders. No new leads, no new clues of value, and no plausible explanations were offered in reference to the triple homicides. A core of six from the department's finest homicide detectives were assigned full time to the cases. They met on a regular basis to review and offer expertise and plausible conjectures in reference to their task. This killer was judged to be either extremely talented in planning and committing the foul deeds, or was being blessed with a considerable amount of good fortune during the rampage.

Chapter 53

"GETTING AWAY"

Colerain decided that he needed a few quiet days to himself. He hoped to engage himself in some reflecting and contemplating in reference to the six most recent and complex months of his life. A sketch pad and some drawing implements might also come in handy during his planned three-day stay at Mount Davis State Park. He went online to rent a secluded one-room cabin in a forested area that still maintains an aura of wilderness. Mount Davis is the highest point above sea level in the state of Pennsylvania, at 3,213 feet. He casually packed a canvass bag with a change of clothing, hiking gear and boots, and some easily prepared food and necessary provisions. The log cabin was equipped with a small, natural gas stove for heating and cooking and a mini refrigerator. A toilet and a cold water showering unit provided him the basic of modern amenities. Knowing that the nights would be quite cool, he also took along his Yukon Zone sleeping bag.

His goals for the sabbatical were serenely simple: to get a couple days of rest and relaxation and become involved in some sketching and drawing of the wonders of nature. He informed Gina of his plans and indicated that he would travel with his cell phone if she needed to communicate with him.

Colerain needed to think. All subjects were to be entertained during his planned peace and quiet. Being wealthy meant very little to him. Considering the devastation of losing both of his parents to actions in the Amazon, he felt that their deaths could have been avoided. His invested funds grew, practically unnoticed. He entered into a career in the financial realm, not because of any profound interest, but because he found it financially prosperous. Occasionally, he would dip into his growing fortune for the purchase of his condominium, a cash-only transaction for a new vehicle, or a vacation.

Within the past few years he began to donate anonymously to a list of chosen and select charities. Recently, he donated fifty thousand dollars toward the construction of a new and spacious animal shelter-kennel facility. The shelter recently declared itself a no-kill facility and it needed a new building for its expansion of care and preservation capabilities. Colerain was extremely generous with legitimate and sincere organizations, which he fastidiously investigated. When he noted a need by a struggling yet hardworking family, he donated to them with little or no fanfare. He relished his giving and helping, always feeling most comfortable cloaking his generosity.

Chapter 54

"PROVIDING AID AND ASSISTANCE"

He awoke at dawn to a brilliantly glowing sun in a cloudless eastern sky. He felt the coolness of the morning, knowing the temperature had probably descended into the mid-forties during the night. A four-cup pot of hot coffee and an onion bagel with saltless peanut butter provided enough fuel to begin his trek to the summit of Mount Davis. Cargo shorts and its many compartments held his Swiss army officer's knife, a banana and granola bar, his cell phone, digital camera, and a GPS device. He wore a windbreaker suit jacket wrapped around his waist, and upon his head he placed a black University of Colorado baseball cap. Before departing he filled a quart-sized canteen with fresh water from the spigot at the rear of his cabin.

Besides reaching the highest point above sea level in Pennsylvania, he had hoped to locate a crystal-clear mountain pool located at around three thousand feet. The year-round temperature of the pool's waters was somehow naturally maintained at about forty degrees Fahrenheit. The body of water possessed a bubbling cauldron emitting cake batter like sand that rose out of the pool's bed. Maintaining his walking and climbing balance with a recently carved walking stick, he energetically followed marked paths littered with watermelon-sized rocks and boulders.

Suddenly, pausing in his ascent, he became aware of a shrill call emanating from an area directly above him, which he estimated was about one hundred yards in the distance. The cry suggested an animal, maybe a panther involved in pursuit of its daily bread. Seconds later a cry—a louder and more desperate version—this one sounding decidedly more human, sent Colerain into a scrambling climb along the path in front of him.

With his heart pounding and his throat burning, he climbed those approximately one hundred yards in a sixty seconds or so. Mentally, he envisioned a scene where a wildcat was savagely attacking a camper or hiker. Another cry, this time with the word "help" clearly projected, brought him into a clearing where he caught sight of two women in a state of total undress. Possibly, the two women had selected a secluded site to enjoy each other's pleasures. As they were undressing, possibly in excited anticipation for lovemaking, they failed to pay attention to their immediate surroundings and one of the women was bitten by a serpent. The rattlesnake must have been sunning its five-foot length upon some flat rocks seeking warmth from the rising sun.

The woman, Karen Wooltane, had been struck midway up the back of her right calf. The viper had apparently bitten her within the past minute or so, about the time that he had first heard her shrieks for assistance. The two women were rightly terrified of the bite and its possible dire consequences. Time was of the essence and maintaining a calm demeanor would be key factors in combating the effects of the snakebite's venom.

He politely suggested to the women to put their clothing back on and to immediately stop shouting and slow down the movements of their bodies. Somewhat embarrassed about the realization of their exposure, they made awkward attempts to cover themselves. Colerain cautiously approached them and made an authoritative suggestion about needing to regain their composure.

He stated, "Ladies, let's not allow that venom any more opportunities to move too rapidly through her system," as he pointed to the victim. "Why don't you both finish dressing and limit your movements to ones that are of necessity." Then, he turned, facing away, so that he would not become an audience to their efforts.

Ms. Wooltane and Ms. Christy Linheart sobbed their reply, "Okay, mister, okay."

After the women finished dressing, he reassured them that he would assist the pair in reaching the park ranger facility for immediate treatment of the snakebite. He estimated that returning down the trail might take about thirty minutes. He confided that he was reasonably sure that the park rangers would have the correct anti-venom available. Snakebites were a fairly common occurrence in this isolated mountainous area.

When the women indicated that they were ready to travel, Colerain carefully picked up Karen and gently slung her over his right shoulder. He kept reminding himself to use the fireman's carry, or that he was carrying a 120-pound sack of potatoes. With her head facing a backward direction, he maintained visual contact with her lover, Christy. She kept reassuring her partner to remain calm and that she would be okay. The women expressed their love for each other and profusely thanked the sweating human cargo-bearing Colerain. He silently wished that they would embrace silence to allow him to concentrate on not losing his passenger to the unsure footing of the trail.

His calves and thighs burned and were gripped with a constant cutting ache as he continued the demanding descent. Occasionally, he needed to stop and lean his side against a large rock formation or against the trunk of a tree to gain a few seconds of relief. The total descent took nearly thirty-five minutes and when the trio got to within two hundred yards of the ranger station, he suggested to Christy that she should sprint the final distance to the outpost. She was to provide the staff with a heads-up about the incoming snakebite victim.

Two rangers saw the trio and ran ahead of the exhausted Christy and joined Colerain and his passenger. She was gingerly placed upon the ground in a sitting position while tightly continuing to hold the hand of her rescuer. The anti-venom serum was injected into her bared right bicep by one caregiver after the other ranger cleaned and bandaged the wound site. An emergency call had already requested a tri-med helicopter evacuation flight to a nearby medical facility for further treatment and examination. Both of the women had regained their composure and were somewhat reassured by the emergency treatment. The glistening tears that flowed down their cheeks from their blue eyes were now tears of relief and appreciation.

One of the attending rangers filled out the required forms with information provided by Christy Linheart and Colerain Pike. Colerain relished the sincere gratitude from the two women and it warmed him. He felt very pleased and satisfied about his intervention and efforts.

He waited until the helicopter had lifted off and cleared the treeline before he stopped waving vigorously to the passengers. He casually walked back to his cabin and greedily drained the now warm quart of water from his canteen. He removed his hiking boots, lay down on his sleeping bag-covered cot, and sunk into a restful and unbroken twelve-hour-long sleep. It was as fine a period of rest as he had ever experienced.

Chapter 55

"CALMING THOUGHTS DENIED"

He awoke, thoroughly well rested and as hungry as a black bear awakening from a hundred days of winter hibernation. He walked the quarter mile from his rustic cabin to the state park's only diner: a concrete block structure humorously named Ptomaine Jacks. After ordering the mountain logger's breakfast from Jack's paper menu, he sipped black coffee from a stained ceramic mug and opened up a copy of the area's daily morning newspaper.

The *Montane Standard-Herald* featured an article about yesterday's snakebite victim and the stranger who rescued her. The article was rather well written and seemed to accurately portray the events that had occurred atop Mount Davis. Listed in the story were the names of the individuals involved, including the man who performed the heroic feat, a Mr. Rand Tillman. He was proclaimed a modern-day hero for carrying Ms. Karen Wooltane down the mountain to safety for prompt medical treatment. He enjoyed the sound of the name that he had supplied to the newspaper staff writer, Rand Tillman. It simply rolled from his lips.

After reading the article Colerain welcomed the sense of contentment that was his reward for his role in assisting the two women. Of course, remembering the sight of the women, nearly nude, also produced masculine reactions that he found pleasurable. He was a person who, long ago, seemed able to extinguish any lingering negative perceptions in reference to homosexuals. People, and their choices in life—particularly if they do no harm—are entirely their own business. Gay people, whom he believed comprised at least 3 to 5 percent of the population of the United States (approximately ten million individuals), should be afforded all rights and protections given to all other citizens. He knew several teachers, artists, lawyers, and investors who were gay. Usually, their homosexuality was last on the list of their personal attributes or abilities. He correctly sensed that when he met or noticed men who were unusually attractive facially or even pretty, they were, in fact, gay men. With respect to women, he usually could not determine their homosexuality easily, except for the butch-type woman who openly exhibited her preferences.

His logger's breakfast was a bounty of fats and carbs that he usually avoided. The three scrambled eggs fried in butter, four strips of bacon, a hill of fried hash brown potatoes, and two flapjacks with strawberry-maple syrup were consumed greedily. Along with all the hot coffee that he could drink, he believed that the price of $3.95 for the meal was highway robbery. He left Corrine, his lean gray-haired waitress, a ten-dollar bill, providing her with a tip of $5.81 on a tab, with tax, that required $4.19. He did consider leaving her more when he overheard her telling another customer that she was separated from her drunken pig of a husband and that she was solely responsible for their four children. But something about her exceptionally foul mouth prevented him from extending his generosity.

As he returned to his cabin to gather his belongings and prepare for his checkout, a disturbing mantra began to spoil his state of comfort. The words "save a woman or kill a woman" began to circulate like coiled razor wire being pulled through his mind. He never experienced murderous thoughts or savagery when it came to his three victims. He simply felt that it was necessary to perform his acts to rid himself of their unrelenting presence. These thoughts only involved the four women who had rejected and then disposed of him. Tiumes Maggic's image reappeared into his visual awareness. Her mannerisms, facial features, skin, and body played before him in micro detailed sequences. He searched for some all-powerful hate, but he could not locate any. He questioned himself with a repeated sentence. Does he really need to extinguish her life light? The other three women were dead, buried, or cremated, He probably would never be held accountable for their deaths. He was confident that he would never reveal a clue or have a weak moment of revelation. His everlasting solitary secret, and the fact that dead women are not able to tell tales, was his fortress of protection.

Chapter 56

"THEY CALL IT POLICE WORK"

The commander of the Taviston Municipal Police Force, Gregor V. Wallace, was a thirty-one-year veteran of law enforcement. He had filled an ascending order of positions during his long and decorated career. He began as a beat patrolman, rose to the rank of sergeant, then lieutenant, captain, and finally, four years ago, was selected and sworn in as the city police commander and chief. In time, he had earned universal respect from the men and women that he commanded. He was considered to be a fair and impartial leader who consistently surrounded himself with the highest-quality subordinates no matter their background or heritage.

He had invited homicide detectives Fredericka Green and Ricardo Stuart to an 8 a.m. meeting at his office on the last day of August. On this particular Thursday, the daytime temperature was expected to creep into the low nineties with rarely reached levels of humidity. He was simmering, just below boil, in reference to the three related strangulation murders and the apparent inability to make progress toward solving them. The meeting was for him to gain information about any current progress made in their investigation.

As expected by Commander Wallace, the two detectives arrived ten minutes early for the meeting. The detectives were led into his commendation-and-citation-adorned office and asked to take a seat in leather upholstered swivel chairs.

After a few moments of cordial chatting and catching up about life in general, he began the meeting.

"Detectives Green and Stuart, I am requesting a current update of the ongoing investigations of the three seemingly related and unsolved murders that have plagued our fair city," he explained.

Fredericka cleared her throat and offered the following information. "We have been able to determine some general physical information about this killer. All three victims were between 5 feet 3 inches and 5 feet 5 inches tall. We know because of the angle that the wire, the murder instrument, which was tilted slightly upward, indicating that his height had to be greater than the height of any of the women. Also, with the assistance of a computer program that we downloaded from the San Antonio, Texas Police Department, we were able to determine, based upon his 11 1/2 shoe size, that the average man with that foot size has a better than 90 percent chance of being between 5 feet 11 inches and 6 feet 1 inch feet tall."

"So," Commander Wallace interjected, "there is a good probability that our perpetrator is in that height range. Interesting." He continued, "Have we found out anything about the wire that he uses to kill?"

Detective Stuart replied, "Based upon microscopic tissue studies of the strangulation sites, the wire was most likely similar to a 14 gauge wire."

"Can you explain the difference in wire thickness or gauge to me?" asked the commander.

"Yes, sir, I can," replied Daniels. "The 12 and 14 gauge wires are commonly seen in electrical house wire. Those are pretty thick and not easily bendable; besides, those thicknesses are also not very flexible. The higher the number given to wire, the thinner the wire. For example, a 22 gauge wire might be used as a guitar string or higher sound-emitting piano key wire. Sgt. Mike Kingerski, over at scientific processing, believes that the wire used here may be of a twisted cable-like construction with a thickness of 14 gauge, strong enough and flexible enough to have been used in these crimes."

"Any other physical evidence gathered, say, with the three pairs of gift shoewear?" Chief Wallace inquired.

"Sir, we were able to find microscopic cotton fibers in the two pairs of boots," Fredericka answered.

"Cotton, what, from socks?' he asked.

She replied, "No, fibers from cotton balls, you know, like cosmetically used cotton balls from any home or medicine chest."

"Why might there have been cotton balls in his boots?" the commander asked with a quizzed look upon his face.

"I don't know, but my grandmother always put a couple of cotton balls into her dress shoes because she said that her feet perspired a lot," she explained.

"Well, interesting thought, I guess," he commented. "How about personal relationships or troubles of that nature with any of the women?" he continued.

"Erica Stamcic did have one individual at Labine-Mizell Investment Securities that wasn't too fond of her," offered Detective Stuart. "One investor, Mark Stepknot, was overheard on a couple of occasions referring to her as a 'dried-up spinster bitch' because she had requested that he refrain from over-socializing with two of her married secretaries. Apparently his advances were making the women uncomfortable in the workplace. He told Ms. Stamcic to mind her own fucking business. Mr. Stepknot is 6 feet 4 inches tall and weighs well over three hundred pounds, and with, I might add, size 14 feet. A former college football player who considers himself some sort of ladies' man. Further investigation revealed that he was in Hubbard, Ohio, with family for the Thanksgiving holiday when Ms. Stamcic was murdered."

He continued, "Ms. Jodie Brooktide had no interpersonal or relationship problems as far as we can tell. We also attempted to speak to her elderly mother, but apparently her dementia has worsened, and she currently resides in a full-care nursing facility and is rapidly losing her ability to communicate."

Detective Green then spoke of the third woman. "In reference to Anye Santillo, we were able to speak with the other two Jaybelles, Sandy Burton and Callie Foiles, on a number of occasions. They drew complete blanks when it came to remembering anyone who posed a threat or caused a problem for any of the three musicians. The trio had worked and toured together for two years and they could not recall anyone who held a grudge for any of them from anywhere."

Then looking at her commander, she added, "At Basil's nightclub where the Jaybelles were scheduled to perform before Ms. Burton became ill, there was one ignorant and inebriated member of the audience who aggressively complained about the postponement of the concert. In a vile and threatening manner, she sprayed her ire upon the three ladies, particularly at Ms. Santillo. That large and obnoxious woman, Torley Summers, was arrested for public intoxication and lewdness for exposing her breasts to arresting police officers. But she did spend the next two nights in a lockup until her boyfriend posted a straight $2,000 bail bond request."

"Well, thank you, Detectives, I appreciate both of your contributions to this updating. And please keep me informed regularly of any new information pertinent to this investigation," concluded the somber-faced commander.

"You're welcome, sir, we will," came the simultaneous reply from the two detectives.

Chapter 57

"THE OPENING OF ANOTHER SCHOOL YEAR"

For the opening of the 2012-13 school year, all district employees were required to attend a meeting to identify the goals and themes for the new school year. Dr. Jock Mason-Puddle had recently been hired as the new superintendent of the Taviston Public School System. He was selected from a group of eleven prospective candidates, culled from a national search process conducted by a committee of civic, legal, and educational leaders. Dr. Arturo Menendez had retired in June after leading the school district brilliantly during the previous nine years. He was well liked and extremely competent in leading the district into the "no child left behind" era. He would be greatly missed by the Taviston educational community.

The hiring of Dr. Mason-Puddle came as a surprise to many of the district's teachers and administrators. He was young, 38 years old, and with no previous experience at directing an established 20,000-student member school district. He was well spoken, handsome, with impressive public appeal, and had received his doctorate in education from Cornell University. Several members of the search committee were said to believe that the time for better local and regional publicity for the district had arrived. The charisma of the new superintendent and his professed willingness to work with the powers-that-be was a huge factor in his selection.

All school district employees met for opening day ceremonies and festivities at the City Central Sporting Arena. Every administrator, teacher, counselor, teacher aide, custodian, security force member, office staffer, secretary, and school board member was expected to be in attendance. Of course, all local media from television to radio to Internet personalities were invited to allow for concentrated coverage of the spectacle.

A choir formed from district music teachers performed admirably, singing three numbers, including one that centered upon audience participation. An all-star band of some 200 high school students played several pieces ranging from John Philip Sousa to the *Star Wars* theme. The atmosphere of the arena could have been considered electric.

After the excitement of the opening ceremonies and entertainment, a buzz was still humming through the four-thousand-or-so member audience. That buzz faded quickly when the usual school themes and projections for the new school year droned on endlessly through a blisteringly loud sound system. For some in the massive gathering, an unfolded newspaper, a casual conversation with a neighbor, or an unplanned nap provided some respite from the sheer face of boredom and the audio assault.

Colerain Pike, observer, was still employed part-time to provide investment counseling primarily to teachers and arrived shortly after the program had begun. Unnoticed, he occupied a seat in an upper-level section to the left side of the presenters' platform or staging area. He was totally disinterested in the speech making and considered leaving the festivities considering he was initially unable to locate his target. He was clearly able to see an isolated group of eight young women sitting near the front of the "C" level just below his "D" level perch. Without listening carefully, he found, he was able to hear their conversation even though the sound system blared. There must have been an unseen air current or spacing that permitted their voices to be projected upward to his level. Unexpectedly, one of the young women rose from her seat and announced that she was leaving for home in an attempt to seek some relief from her horrible menstrual cramping. Veteran teacher Tiumes Maggic was starting her eleventh year with the district. Her face displayed the unpleasant indicators of irritation and discomfort. Colerain recognized those facial expressions. He had experienced the mood changes and irritability that came with non-estrus during their relationship.

"Unbelievable good fortune," he thought, as he casually watched Tiumes leave the sporting arena. He was quite certain that she was, in fact, heading home. He knew of the extent of her extremely uncomfortable periods. He waited fifteen minutes before he casually got up from his seat and moved toward an isolated exit. Without being noticed, he walked quickly to that lane through the arena's concourse and departed through a seldom-used side door that was primarily used for the delivery of concessions. He had parked on a side street, about four city blocks from the facility. He walked briskly, feeling confident that his short stay and hasty departure went completely unnoticed. Within minutes he was inside the cabin of his truck and beginning the twenty-minute drive to 1141 Rosedale Street.

Colerain was wearing lightweight black slacks and a short sleeved polo-type shirt, the color of which could be described as a hint of gray. He wore black leather Italian sandals, woven with openings, and, of course, no socks. He removed the sandals and placed them on the passenger-side front seat and put on a pair of size 11/12 black beach flip-flops. When he arrived into the neighborhood of the Rosedale Street address, he parked his vehicle and slipped into a virtually weightless black leather sport coat and prepared to don a pair of tight-fitting black leather gloves. Intuitively, he checked the pockets of his jacket to be certain that they contained the necessary implements to complete his predetermined task.

Confidence surfaced swiftly into his planning because he was very familiar with, and knew in great detail, the layout and floor plan of Tiumes Maggic's home. The private front porch with its drooping canvass awning would contribute nicely to his need for the maximum required seclusion. Hopefully, he thought, his visit could be completed in the ten or so minutes similar to the time that three other fateful meetings had needed.

The temperature on this August day was expected to surge into the low nineties. With the humidity levels already high, and the air devoid of any breeze, he listened to a weather report on his truck radio. It was at 84 degrees at 10:00 a.m. He realized that a strenuous and taxing physical effort would have to be undertaken to complete his task successfully. He also recalled that 1141 Rosedale Street did not have central air-conditioning.

Chapter 58

"NOT BUSINESS AS USUAL"

Tiumes arrived at her home and parked her 2001 Toyota Camry in a vacant parking spot directly across the street from her front porch. After entering through the front door, she set her deadbolt lock that Colerain had installed for her years ago. She lay her small leather purse, keys, and sunglasses upon the black marble top of the kitchen island. In her bedroom, she quickly changed into nylon forest green-colored running shorts and a white tank top. She carelessly tossed her slacks, pink short-sleeved blouse, white bra, and thong panties unto an antique Hitchcock-style chair that was positioned next to her five-drawer dresser. Then she plopped herself face down upon her queen-sized bed.

Within seconds her doorbell rang once, and five seconds later, two more times. The harsh, blaring sound grated upon her already challenged nerves and increased her already high level of irritation.

She mumbled out loud to herself, "Who the hell can that be?" Then, in a somewhat restrained voice, she called out, "Okay, I'm coming."

She slid open the deadbolt without asking who was there, and opened the door to its fullest extent, causing her sleeping midnight-black cat Nitro to leap from his comfortable resting chair and exit the kitchen into the hallway toward a bedroom.

Upon recognizing Colerain, she demanded, "What do you want? What are you doing at my door?" The tone of her voice dripped with copious amounts of irritation and toxic surliness.

He calmly replied, "Believe it or not, I was following your directive from years ago to retrieve my three coffee table-sized art books that I left here."

Tiumes let her hand fall from the open front door and allowed him to enter. He deftly closed the door with his left foot as she turned slowly away from him.

While turning, she uttered a comment, laced with disgusting intonations. She commanded, "Wait here, I'll get the stupid things for you."

Just as she was completing that sentence, Colerain's gloved hands had already removed the wire and wrapped it around her willowy throat. He yanked and twisted her body into a position directly in front of and facing away from him. With his powerful arms and hands, he tightened his grip with choking action and began to crush her cartilaginous larynx and restrict the flow of air into her lungs.

As he exerted another, even more powerful, pull upon the wire, he matter-of-factly commented to Tiumes, "The time has come, young lady, to get you out of my head."

After one final pull and twenty-second hold, her body sagged and began to fall back toward Colerain. Bracing her body effortlessly against his left hip, he returned the wire to his right jacket pocket. He gently laid Tiumes atop the highly polished laminated wood flooring between the kitchen island and her oversized black toned, side-by-side refrigerator. He removed her running shorts and tank top, neatly folded them, and set them upon the center island next to her purse, keys, and sunglasses.

As he positioned himself, kneeling next to the lifeless body, he heard a slight, fleeting sound, which caused him to immediately pause and listen. That must have been Nitro, he thought. Maybe that feline can call 911. Colerain placed Tiumes' arms alongside her body, noting that her breasts barely moved and appeared to be like soft mounds atop her chest. Her pubic hair was already cleanly shaved in the bikini style that he preferred. While he was repositioning a few hair strands that had fallen across her face to completely expose her pleasing facial features, he made the decision to close her horror-filled and slightly bulging eyes. The presentation of her body needed to be as dignified as the others.

He removed the black marker pen and was set to begin his drawing. He felt a drop or two of perspiration beginning to bead upon his forehead, needing to be careful not to allow a drop of his sweat to fall upon the wooden kitchen flooring. Obviously, that sample could be gleaned as forensic or DNA evidence by the legion of homicide investigators who would be shortly converging upon this scene. He began to draw the profile of a man in the area between her petite breasts, when again, he was aware of a slight sound or movement in another section of the house. That damn cat, I hope, he thought.

The drawing upon her tanned skin was approximately eight inches high and six inches wide. He highlighted some areas with his color marking pens, this drawing emphasizing the bright yellow marker. Alongside the drawing, he tagged the words “no mas” in the previously used script.

All drawing items were returned to the left pocket of his jacket.

He looked at the body of his former lover and then at a kitchen wall clock that depicted a cartoon character named Felix the Cat, whose tail was ticking back and forth. Felix indicated that it was 10:58 a.m., and he realized that he had been with Tiumes for eight minutes. With gloved hand, he open the front door, stepped through, and quietly closed the door behind him. Tiumes Maggic was 34 years old.

He momentarily stood under the protection of the awning on the front porch, then glanced to his right then left and finally across the street. Confident that his departure would be clean, seeing no one, he stepped off of the porch, turned to the right and calmly walked the two blocks to a side street where his pick-up truck was waiting. He felt fortunate that he did not see or pass another individual during his stroll.

Back inside his vehicle, he removed the flip-flops, wiped them off with common rubbing alcohol and inserted them into a plastic grocery bag. Can't leave any DNA from sweat, he reminded himself. He took off his jacket, leaving on his leather gloves for driving, and slipped back into his comfortable leather sandals while he began searching for a flip-flop drop-off location. He spied a police K-9 SUV vehicle parked near the side entrance of Cisternos Sub & Pizza shop. Hmm, he thought, maybe some men in blue were in the process of obtaining some complimentary lunches. I'll bet the owner, Rico Cisternos, is delighted to provide them with a hoagie, calzone, or two if they keep an extra watchful eye upon his thriving enterprise.

The huge German shepherd police officer/canine American was waiting patiently for his partners in the rear caged area of the SUV. Colerain noticed that the vehicle's front passenger-side window was completely open. During his drive-by he deftly tossed the plastic bag containing the size 11 1/2 flip-flops onto the front seat. No human witnessed the toss, only the canine American, and he paid little attention or regard to the bag's entrance into the public service vehicle.

Colerain drove away, planning to stop somewhere for an early lunch. He immediately began to think about getting something distinctly Italian.

Chapter 59

"MOUNT RUSHMORE"

Detectives Fredericka Green and Ricardo Stuart received the call reporting a possible homicide at 1141 Rosedale Street. The central police dispatch center delivered the call in code by asking any responders if they had ever visited Mount Rushmore, the national monument in southwestern South Dakota. Rushmore corresponded to the four United States presidents whose sculptural portraits are carved into the mountainside at the site. Misters Washington, Jefferson, Lincoln, and T. Roosevelt were used to relate to the number of single white females who have now apparently been strangled in similar fashion. Initial reports by officers first on the scene seemed to confirm that scenario to permit that dreaded code to be issued.

The code was necessary because the general public was legally entitled to complete access to law enforcement transmissions over all available radio frequencies. To be honest, many in law enforcement believed, it was insane that our legal system offered criminals and individuals information that would provide those law breakers possible access to policing and security information.

A 911 call had been reportedly made by a ranting and possibly seriously confused woman, who spoke from a public telephone in a Foodpark grocery store. The call was received at 11:30 and police officers were at the crime scene slightly before 11:50 a.m. securing the premises. Soon, detectives Green and Stuart were pulling their black unmarked Ford Taurus up to the curb at 1141 Rosedale. The detectives literally sprang from their vehicle, leaving the red rotating roof-mounted light blinking continuously. They were relieved and pleased to see that four uniformed officers were already at the scene and functioning.

"What do we have here, Officer Portermein?" asked Fredericka as she approached the front porch and door.

He calmly answered, "Deceased white/Asian woman, I'd say, mid-thirties, and she appears to have been garroted."

"Christ," implored Detective Stuart. "I wonder if it's the same bastard killing again? Is there a drawing?"

"Yes, a drawing on her chest area," replied Officer Sali DeWitt.

Upon the completion of their review and investigation of the now all-too-familiar crime scene, the detectives were able to note that the same exact indicators appeared to be present, probably linking this murder to the three previous crimes. Everything seemed to have been repeated: a strangled, nude, attractive woman posed exactly as the others, a drawing of the profile of a man upon her chest, the words "no more" (no mas) written in Spanish on her chest, the victim's clothing neatly folded and placed together, and no apparent sign of struggle with nothing knocked over, broken, or displaced.

A general police inquiry followed the initial investigation with its all-encompassing procedures, The scene and victim were photographed, dusted, and combed for prints and DNA examples; general and relational canvasses were conducted; interviews with colleagues, friends, and family members were made; and detailed and far-reaching background checking was initiated. This latest victim was a high school teacher who had many friends and acquaintances, no obvious enemies, and a boyfriend, Marvel Strothers, who had an air-tight alibi. Also, the movements and activities of Ms. Tiumes Maggic during her final forty-eight hours had been well documented.

There appeared to be no links or connections between the four victims who appeared to have died in the same exact manner. As far as the investigation could determine, the four women never met or even attended the same event or gathering.

"Random, fucking random," intoned Detective Green. "Is this bastard going to stop? We need to come up with a concise and detailed plan to protect all of the women in our communities, or at least all of the single ones. Shit, I'm single, what do I do if he comes after me?" she continued with a shudder.

Chapter 60

"THE FOURTH PAIR"

"What the hell is this?" growled second-year canine police officer Westford Laker as he opened the passenger door of their SUV. Officer Laker grabbed the blue plastic grocery bag, reached into it, and pulled out a pair of black flip-flops.

"What size are those shoes?" queried his veteran partner, Reed Betancourt.

"Ah, 11/12, the tag says. Why?" questioned Westford.

"Oh my God!" Betancourt exclaimed. "Some guy has been going around killing women and drawing pictures on their bodies and has been leaving shoes around that the police can find. He has left three pairs of shoes that were traced to three murder scenes and he kind of gives the footwear to the police. Oh man! You touched the shoes and the bag. You probably contaminated them. I wonder if the science lab people can lift his prints or something off of them? We better get these flip-flops turned into the homicide department."

"Hey Raven, good boy. Did you see anyone put these shoes into the vehicle?" Reed Betancourt asked the 115-pound German shepherd. Raven loudly barked twice, indicating to his handler that he was ready to resume police work. It is too bad that humans are not able to understand the communicative skills of animals. As with the lack of importance or effort in many other mammal-to-human relationship studies, it will probably take at least another fifty years before humans lower themselves to begin to understand the language-using abilities of dogs and cats.

Chapter 61

"SHE FOUND OUT"

Ria Rangeview was no longer capable of waiting patiently for her husband Miguel to come home from rehearsal in time for a planned candlelit dinner. The Taviston Symphony Orchestra was preparing for the opening performance of its fall concert series. They would be performing the sensual and hot-blooded music from the production known to classical music aficionados as *The Hermanos of the Water Caves.* Miguel had curtly indicated to Ria, on a couple of occasions, that rehearsals were often extended by an hour or two because the music was very challenging to play.

Her carefully planned and meticulously prepared dinner was basically ruined by the two-hour passing of the appointed dinner hour. The homemade chicken cacciatore, one of her specialties based upon a recipe created by her grandmother, was losing its sumptuous sauce. The carefully sliced white meat chicken, sweet onions, fresh mushrooms, crisp celery, vine plucked tomatoes, and assortment of spices with a smattering of red table wine were drying out. The repeated warming and reheating had thoroughly damaged the enticing taste of the lovingly prepared dish. Ria had uncorked a twenty-five-dollar bottle of Beaujolais well over an hour ago and had already disgustedly consumed two large glasses of the fruit of the vines. She was experiencing a heady wine buzz and became more pissed off with each passing minute with another instance of her husband's chronic tardiness. He had indicated that he would arrive home at eight-ish and that he was looking forward to dinner and an evening together with Ria. The wall clock in their hall foyer had just emitted its chimes, proclaiming that the ten o'clock hour had arrived. Ria turned off the flame under the warming burner and viciously tossed a stainless steel slotted spoon against the ceramic splash guard behind the kitchen sink.

She grabbed her house and car keys and her smallish carrying purse as she decided to walk the two blocks to the neighborhood bar and grill known as the Oasis. Loudly slamming the front door of condo unit number 309, she descended three flights of brightly lit stairs and then walked through the exit doors of the Burley Avenue Condominium. Enraged, she walked briskly for about a city block when she noticed two men getting into a parked, silver Honda accord. She immediately thought she recognized her husband, Miguel, as one of the two men sliding into the vehicle.

She walked closely alongside of the Japanese import and peered into the front seat through the passenger-side window. It was shockingly obvious to her that one of the men was beginning to perform an act of fellatio upon his companion who had a head of thick, dark, shoulder-length hair. The toe tapper lifted his head in an apparent attempt to drink in a lungful of fresh air when she sickeningly recognized her husband Miguel Rangeview. She startled the two men by violently kicking at the passenger front door panel. Shocked and frightened, they looked at the kicking woman and abruptly ended their activity. Miguel felt all of the color drain from his face as he opened the car door and attempted to exit from the vehicle.

"Honey," he pleaded, "we need to talk about some things. Please, please, let me talk to you? I will explain everything in God-fearing honesty. I promise you."

"How could you?" she screamed "Why didn't you just tell me that you were gay, instead of me finding you acting like some common, filthy faggot? I fucking hate you. How could you do this to us? And you talked so lovingly about us having children someday." She was unable to control her rage and tears began cascading down Ria's cheeks and depositing their salty contents into the corners of her quivering mouth.

She turned and began to retrace her steps as she headed back toward their building. Miguel followed meekly, pleading with her to stop and begged her to consider the possibility of discussing their lives in a reasonable manner. He made comments about still loving her and promises that he could explain everything.

Chapter 62

"GOLDEN OPPORTUNITY"

Miguel and Ria's neighbors, Leslie and Urbana Butler, resided next door to the young couple in unit 307. Last week the Butlers asked Ria if she would mind keeping an eye on their condo while they spent a week vacationing in North Myrtle Beach, South Carolina. Urbana provided Ria with their vacationing address and cell phone number and asked if their mail could be picked up, and if she could take care of their cat, Mr. Whitcomb. The cat needed to be fed twice a day, given fresh water, and if Ria didn't mind, could she be so kind as to clean the cat's litter box. Pet owners sometimes wonder why their housecat decides to undertake a campaign to use places in the home other than the provided box to deposit their waste material. Obviously, it is because owners are forgetful or unwilling to attend to that chore on a regular schedule. Ria proved to be conscientious in that matter.

As soon as she entered the key into the front door lock, Mr. Whitcomb was there to greet her. He loved to be petted and within seconds, the soothing sound of a feline purring was being emitted from his throat. Sometimes Ria would toss to him a toy mouse that was filled with catnip. That magical cat drug drove the animal into spasms of joy and freestyle cavorting. Mr. Whitcomb would lie on his back, and with all four feet, bat the mouse about the master bedroom. When he would knock the toy under a piece of furniture and couldn't retrieve it, Ria would get on her hands and knees and return it to the playful and appreciative animal. On one occasion, while locating the misplaced toy, she noticed a loaded handgun under the Butlers' bed. She cautiously handled the weapon and allowed herself to become familiar with its mechanisms and then returned it to its hiding place.

Chapter 63

"AN ENDING"

An hour or so after the couple returned to their condo, they were still unable to embark upon a starting point for conversation. Ria was seething, overcome by embarrassment and disgust that proved to be completely paralyzing. Miguel was mournfully silent, somehow trying to create a phrase or comment that could begin his long overdue explanation.

Ria heard Miguel go into their master bedroom bathroom. When she walked silently into the room, she noticed him sitting upon the toilet, holding his head in what appeared to be trembling hands. Boldly she approached him and stood about four feet in front of her seated husband. He looked up at her with his moistened eyes, pleading while she smiled wickedly down upon him. From behind her back, she produced the borrowed nine millimeter Glock semi-automatic handgun. She shot him from point-blank range three times. The first bullet struck him in the area of his heart, the second discharge was aimed at his groin, and the third directly into the middle of his forehead. Instantly, crimson colors covered his white T-shirt and canary yellow boxer shorts. Thrown back against the toilet tank, he did not lose his seat, but from the credit card-sized opening in the back of his head, his brain matter and other human tissues were splattered against the tile wall surface, glass shower door, and the full-length mirror attached to it.

Still carrying the handgun, Ria, without remorse, walked calmly back into the dining room, took her seat, and poured herself a third glass of wine. While savoring the wine, she thoughtlessly ate two homemade dinner breadsticks. The humming of the slowly rotating ceiling fan caught her attention. She looked at it and became transfixed. As she continued to watch the four flat blades rotate, she placed the barrel of the handgun into her thirty-three-year-old mouth and, with steady continuous pressure, depressed the trigger.

Murder-suicide, read the report. A young and attractive woman blew her husband away with three shots from a Glock nine and then ate the gun herself.

Chapter 64

"FRUITLESS INVESTIGATING"

Police Commander Gregor V. Wallace was ready to explode. His agitated and aggravated state neared an epic level when he received the information surrounding the three deaths that had occurred on his watch in the past twenty-four hours. During this one malignant day, the number of killings committed in the city of Taviston had gone up by 50 percent, from the unacceptable six to the unheard-of total of nine.

Speaking directly to Detectives Green and Stuart, even though there were a dozen investigators surrounding him, he plowed through the latest information related to the deaths. "Young couple, probably a murder suicide, with the wife as the shooter. The murder weapon was recovered with at least four rounds fired. Seems pretty cut and dry. Apparently the young woman discovered that her husband was actively gay, caught him in an act, and she went ballistic. And the other, a thirty-four-year-old white/Asian female teacher, who was strangled in her home. It looks as though that murderous bastard got his fourth. Drawing on the torso, 'no mas' graffiti, clothing piled up neatly, body positioning the same as the others, and of course, no fucking evidence or clues. Was this Maggic woman molested?"

"No, sir," Detective Green answered.

"What about the trace of blood on her inner upper thigh and the microscopic amount of blood on the hardwood kitchen floor?" he demanded.

"Apparently, the medical examiner has determined that she was in the middle of having her period and had recently removed her insert," responded Fredericka.

"Shit," he said, "shit."

"Stuart, was there anything different about this fourth murder scene? Do you believe that this was done by the same perpetrator? Any changes in methods, any different information uncovered? Tell me, Detective, tell me," he ordered in a tone of sheer frustration.

"Sir, we had six investigating detectives on the scene who are all very familiar with these related cases. We believe that nothing was overlooked. Everything appeared to be the same as the three previous episodes. Same everything, same damn everything," he replied.

"What about the drawing, or drawings? Does it look like anybody? Should we be looking for men who look like the men portrayed in the drawings?" the commander asked no one in particular.

"It could be anyone or no one. Hundreds of guys look like what is depicted in those drawings. First a long-haired guy on victim number one, then hair combed behind his ears with a short full beard, then on the third woman shorter hair and a goatee, and on this woman real short hair and just some chin hair. Maybe he is aging or evolving, or maybe, he is just simply fucking around with everyone, who knows?" offered Fredericka Green.

"What's this I heard about shower shoes or flip-flops, as you call them, and a K-9 patrol wagon?" the commander asked calmly.

"Yes, sir, we got them, size 11/12, but very clean with no prints or DNA except from the rookie police officer who found them in a plastic bag on the front seat of the canine unit vehicle," offered Detective Ricardo Stuart.

Chapter 65

"NEWSWORTHY"

Colerain had always made a conscientious effort to remain current in relation to world, national, and local news developments. On a daily basis he read the local Taviston *Lone Telegraph* and digested the *New York Times* and the *Washington Post* via the Internet. He enjoyed the most highly circulated weekly news journals and had a particular liking for *Time* magazine.

On the local level, the fourth victim of the so-called No mas Murderer dominated all aspects of the local media. From call-in discussions on talk show radio programs to Taviston's two major television stations, including public service broadcasting. The written media horde was writing about the murders from realistic, sensationalized, and distorted angles. Theories, blame, and conjecture of the crimes had, of course, driven up the levels of circulation and advertisements. The stories of the murders were solid, old-fashioned indicators of good business.

The four apparently related slayings had also garnered the attention of national media outlets, including CNN, Fox News, and the three major affiliates of ABC, CBS, and NBC. Talk and theories on the street about the murders was spreading as rapidly as the wind-driven wildfires of Southern California. Legal and illegal handgun purchases were said to be skyrocketing. Women were choosing to have their homes relocked and reinforced. They were clearing out the kennels of the Humane Society of all of the large dogs housed there and demanding more protection and surveillance from the now inept-labeled overpaid police. Panic seemed to have set in, considering the number of murders and their unsolved status. The citizens of Taviston were demanding resolution of this heinous crime spree.

Colerain did not derive satisfaction or perverse pleasure from the four murders attaining national media attention. The title "No Mas Murderer" or the "Wire Strangler" seemed so overused and lacking in interest or originality. Within himself he secretly wished that he could inform law enforcement and its investigators that the extended killing period had ended and that there would be no further victims. In a way, he wanted the general population to have their fears and trepidations of more killings to be extinguished. Realistically, he knew that he would never reveal the slightest detail of his activities to any other living human. No one else will ever need to die, at least not by his hands. He confidently believed that his deeds were carried out so carefully and with extraordinary good fortune that he would never be suspected of, or held accountable for, committing them.

During those two days since the death of Tiumes Maggic, he felt for the first time in his life perfectly at peace within himself. No woman was in his head. He possessed or carried no sense or feeling of any degree of guilt. He believed that his guiltlessness would be considered inhumane or sociopathic by almost all in society, but he considered himself humane and by no means a sociopath. By his thought processing, although obscure, he saw the women as not murdered but only eliminated. Normally that thinking would be obscene, but he believed it to be reasonable.

In a related matter, he perceived the deaths of Ria and Miguel Rangeview to be fortunate related occurrences because they were the only two known individuals who knew of his secretive relationship with a younger woman. Tiumes had chosen to conceal her relationship with Colerain, steadfastly limiting the opportunities for others to see them together in public. It seldom bothered him that Tiumes preferred to keep him entirely to herself. Now he appreciated the control exhibited by his younger lover. Good karma, he reasoned. Or maybe she was just somewhat embarrassed to be that involved with a man who was almost twice her age. Whatever, her behavior should end up contributing to him not being considered as a suspect in her death, because virtually no one was permitted to know of their affair.

If Ria and Miguel had lived, he believed that eventually they may have aided the investigators in linking him to the death of Tiumes Maggic. He realized that intense questioning, multidirectional probing, and an all-encompassing pursuit would have followed. Ultimately, he might have surfaced as a potential suspect and would have been required to produce feasible alibis and DNA samples and be subjected to endless interrogation and testing. The unrelenting investigation methodology could have been used on the artistically talented and physically capable Colerain Pike. He was at peace with the young couple's murder-suicide

Being brought to justice in Pennsylvania, convicted by a jury of his peers of the capital one multiple-murder charges, he was aware that he would receive a death sentence by lethal injection. Appeals could add years to his life in a maximum security restrictive unit, but his day of judgment would arrive when the correct governor took over the mansion in the Keystone State. In his reality, if he made a mistake in revealing any involvement or aspect of the crimes, then and only then could he be considered suspect in those deeds. The investigators didn't even seem close to determining the essentials of the murder weapon.

Mr. Colerain Pike was quite confident that he would be able to live the rest of his natural life free from the tortures of the four women in his head and never fall under any cloak of suspicion for their premature demise. Today would be a good day for him as he looked forward to meeting Gina this evening for dinner and, possibly, some intimacy.

Chapter 66

"THE PASSING OF A NOTE"

Two months had passed since Gina and Colerain had been able to take an opportunity to dine at their favorite restaurant, Zapatas. They planned to meet at 7:00 p.m. and were anticipating a relaxing dining experience outdoors on the restaurant's spacious patio and grotto. Throughout much of September, the weather of Western Pennsylvania has been considered as close to perfect as any climate in the United States. The days are warm, with the sun dominating the nearly cloudless skies. Evenings outdoors are comfortable, usually requiring only a light jacket or sweater. The nights are pleasantly cool, providing the area with comfortable sleeping temperatures. Air conditioners are usually turned off, removed, or quietly forgotten. The harmonious couple had entertained thoughts of dining at the highly rated Mexican restaurant ever since the owner, Diego Vargas-Zapatas, commissioned Colerain to paint a pair of peasant's shoes on a wall of the cantina. He painted a stunningly realistic pair of *zapatos* that were about the size of two six-string guitars. When offered remuneration for his effort, he steadfastly refused.

He located a parking spot about two blocks from his destination. He left the doors of his vehicle unlocked and began his stroll toward the restaurant, planning his arrival for a minute or two before seven o'clock. The sidewalks and avenues in the area were pulsating with vehicle traffic, walkers, shoppers, and many others seeking the myriad of venues for entertainment and dining options. It appeared as though everyone was out enjoying this superb Saturday evening in early September.

Colerain sidestepped a young mother pushing an elaborately constructed child's stroller while the father lovingly carried their two-year-old daughter atop his shoulders. The daddy tugged lightly at the little girl's legs and she squealed loudly with obvious delight. While Colerain gave his immediate attention to the family, a rather smallish figure dressed in a full-length black skirt, a black, long-sleeved jacket, black baseball-styled cap, and sunglasses thrust a white envelope into his right hand. Unconsciously, he accepted the business-sized envelope. Vacationers and tourists who traverse the boulevards of Las Vegas, Nevada or other tourist meccas know how easy it is to accept an entertainment flyer or porno business card from a street ad pusher. That pusher, who is being paid to distribute those coupons and flyers, will flick that card and momentarily catch the attention of the visually overwhelmed walker. Eighty percent of the time, the person affected will accept that ad card and, with a quick examination, will determine that the card promotes an escort service or other form of adult entertainment. A huge segment of the litter on the Las Vegas streets is a result of those advertisements.

A second after he accepted the envelope from the black clad woman, she had already slipped, unseen, into the human congestion. His visual scanning for the woman proved to be unsuccessful. He stared at the unsealed envelope. Several questions began to parade through his mind about this new possession. Anthrax laden? A mistake? A joke? Who is playing around with me? Gina Epki? He stopped walking, stepped backward toward the dark, red-bricked wall of Anderson and Sons, Attorneys-at-Law. Without hesitation he opened the envelope and removed the single sheet of folded white, 8x11-inch paper. A note, printed in black ink, was addressed to him. It read:

> MR. PIKE: I WAS THERE, AT 1141 ROSEDALE, WHEN YOU KILLED TIUMES. YOU HEARD NOISES AND THOUGHT OF HER CAT, NITRO. I ACCIDENTALLY MADE THOSE NOISES (STUPID ME). YOU PUT THE CHOKING WIRE BACK INTO YOUR JACKET POCKET-RIGHT SIDE. I SAW THE WHOLE DEED.
>
> H.M.L.T.

He was staggered by the revelations of those five simple sentences. His body felt as though it was being pummeled by a hostile and powerful opponent. With his back placed firmly against the building's brick wall, he pressed the back of his head to that wall for stability. With sweat beading rapidly upon his face and his heart rate rising uncontrollably, he felt sick to his stomach.

"Are you okay, mister?" asked a tall elderly woman who had stopped when she recognized a fellow human in obvious distress. "Mister, do you want me to summon the EMS or a medical brigade?"

"What, what did you say?" he replied, as he attempted to ascertain the source of the question and gain a semblance of visual focusing.

"Sir, do you need medical attention?" she asked again in a concerned and calming voice.

Thinking quickly on his feet, Colerain responded. "No, thank you, I was just momentarily choking on a piece of hard candy." He coughed twice and added, "No, I'm all right, a little shook up, that's all. Thanks for your concern."

He was embarrassed that he had brought attention to himself and chided himself for displaying that weakness. Now, he hoped that none of his mannerisms or movements would indicate any more of the uncomfortableness that had surged through him. He sensed that the flushing and heat from the rapid rise of his heartbeat and blood pressure were beginning to recede from his pulsating heart.

As he regained his composure, he began to walk the remaining short distance to the restaurant. While he walked he refused to turn his head to scan the crowded walkway for a possible glimpse of the note bearer. Just a few steps away from the entrance to Zapatas, his cell phone vibrated. Reaching into his pocket for the phone, he realized, by scanning the caller ID, that it was Gina calling.

He flipped open the device and offered, "Hello, my sweet Gina."

She responded, slightly out of breath, "Colerain, my darling, I won't be able to meet you for dinner at Zapatas. My sister, Angelica—Angelica Baywright—had just received an alarming telephone call, about ten minutes ago, from a Taviston police investigator from the Narcotics Division. The officer introduced himself as Detective Waseta Talbot, badge number 419. He informed Angelica that her husband, Vincent, had been apprehended along with two other men, at a rest stop on Interstate 80, near the Dubois, Pennsylvania, exit. Vincent is alleged to have been delivering two kilos of heroin to the two New Jersey natives. Thousands of dollars were being exchanged for the two pavement-brick-sized, plastic-wrapped packages."

Angelica was understandably shocked and disturbed and she begged Gina to accompany her to her husband's arraignment.

Colerain stated, quite calmly, "Just go, Gina, support your sister. Call me later or whenever to let me know if I can be of some assistance."

Gina hung up her phone while uttering, "I love you."

Chapter 67

"SWEAT BOX"

He was relieved to be able to avoid his commitment to dinner with Gina. He realized that he might have been challenged to maintain his composure, thus possibly revealing information about his obvious shaken status. He knew that she would cautiously and expertly probe him for an explanation for his unusual behavior. He could not hide much from her. He would be powerless to divert her suspicion about the alterations in his behavior that currently he could not totally control.

Returning to the security of his condominium, he glanced at the blue lighted digital clock of his microwave oven as he walked in the door. It was 7:37 p.m. He handled the remote control and pondered whether to give life to his HD, 42-inch, flat screen television. Instead of pressing the power button, he lay the instrument down upon the uncluttered surface of his 5x2-foot wooden coffee table. As he sunk and slunk lower into the black Corinthian leather surface of his couch, he sensed that his sweating was making his clothing adhere to the rich natural material. He felt moisture collecting under the back of his thighs and unconsciously rubbed that area, then he wiped the collected perspiration from his hands onto the sides of his dress slacks.

He picked up the panic-inducing white envelope, removed the note, and re-read the message carefully. After studying the context, he was convinced that someone had clearly witnessed his killing of Ms. Tiumes Maggic. The letters H.M.L.T. were deeply confusing. Someone's name? A code indicated? The racking of his brain was not able to produce any viable explanation for the puzzling letters. He believed that his arrest was imminent. Four murders, all related, he knew that he would be facing the death penalty as the necessary consequence for his crimes. Overcome by a flash of reality, he decided that he would never extend his life by a costly and plodding series of the customary appeals. He believed that lawyers filled their coffers and the citizens of his Commonwealth would have their taxes wasted by the rigmarole of that unglorified process. He did kill the four women.

In the parlance of the day, he was busted. He decided that he would not attempt to flee the area, hide, or seek unadvised religious sanctuary. He would accept, with dignity, his pending arrest, punishment, and whatever else awaited him.

Again, he thought to himself, "You did kill four worthwhile human beings." Nobody would have thought that they were expendable.

Unexpectedly, an all-encompassing sensation of calmness enveloped him. He removed his shoes and stretched his once-agitated body lengthwise along the softened leather couch. Within a few minutes, he drifted into a state of sound sleep that he rarely experienced. No stages of dreaming or periods of confusing nightmarish sequences interrupted his peaceful state. The rest allowed his beleaguered body to restore and re-energize itself. It was also unusual that he did not have his slumber disturbed by a visit to the bathroom. He slept continuously for twelve consecutive hours and awoke naturally at 8 a.m. the next day. After showering, shaving, and trimming his goatee, he donned an old pair of scuff-around shorts and a black, short-sleeved T-shirt with "I can't be good all of the time" printed upon it.

Wearing a worn pair of navy blue flip-flops, he sauntered outside to retrieve his morning *Lone Telegraph.* While turning to retrace his steps to his opened front door, he noticed an ordinary piece of folded white paper propped under a windshield wiper of his truck. He took possession of the paper and quickened his pace back into his condo, closing the front door in a manner that, in reality, was slamming.

He placed the plastic bag-protected newspaper and the folded white paper atop his kitchen counter and calmly proceeded to make himself some caffeine-rich beverage in his automatic coffee maker. He slid two slices of low-carb wheat bread into the slits of his pop-up toaster and removed two wedges of sliced cantaloupe and some healthy heart spread from the refrigerator. He was famished. The long sleep and the missed dining opportunity left him famished this morning.

"Note: Number #2"
(Fate and circumstance have returned him to this moment)

He was determined to enjoy his morning repast of Colombian coffee, wheat toast, a healthy heart spread, fruit, and daily morning newspaper. He quickly scanned the front and local sections of the newspaper, seeking references to any storylines relating to the recent spate of homicides. Finding no references surprised him. He sipped his coffee and devoured his toast while pondering the following questions. Why were the police not making any announcements about the crimes? Why so hush-hush? When might the authorities pay him that fateful visit? He decided to remain at home and emotionally prepare himself for the inevitable.

With his hunger and thirst satisfied, he finished the second wedge of juicy cantaloupe then unfolded the white sheet of paper revealing a simple, one-line note. The short message, written neatly in black ink, stated:

FOUR KILLED, ONLY ONE BY YOU, SO WHAT?
L.T.

L.T.? Who is this L.T.? I know a Lucerne Thomas and a Leonardis Tasker. Who else? He thought. What the hell does this mean? Puzzled and chagrined, he attempted to put aside the thoughts provoked by the note. Does this person think that I might have killed only one of the four women? Confounded and annoyed with his incompetence at deciphering the notes, he decided to embark upon the mindless task of cleaning his condominium.

He used a Swiffer mop pad to gather the dust colonies living upon his hardwood flooring. He had to replace the soft white pad twice because of an exploding dust bunny population. Two toilet bowls were bleached and scrubbed, carpeting was vacuumed, and all mirrors were cleaned with a solution of vinegar and water wiped with balled-up newspaper to prevent streaking. The cleaning rampage had little or no effect upon his emotional anguish. He endured a three-mile jog at increased degrees of elevation and speeds on his treadmill before he began to experience some lessening of his aggravation. He covered the distance in twenty-eight minutes while wearing a wrist-mounted heart monitor. He was also successful in getting his heart rate up to 140 beats per minute, as recommended by his cardiologist.

After his cleaning and exercise workouts, his hunger returned. He satisfied his need by consuming two large bowls of Gina's homemade beef barley soup that she had provided him at the beginning of the week.

His cellphone vibrated. Gina was calling.

Colerain flipped open his phone and Gina began speaking immediately. "Bad news for Vincent. He is really busted this time, the asshole. The black tar heroin was from Mexico, America's number one supplier nation and source." She added, "He has been involved in an extremely profitable business run by crafty entrepreneurs who recognize that vast market of hundreds of thousands of American users. Vincent saw an opportunity to make huge profits, he thought." Gina paused and then completed the one-sided conversation. "Colerain, my dear, I'm going to stay with Angelica until, at least, tomorrow. Maybe then I can spend an evening with you. Bye, I'll call tomorrow, okay? I love you. Bye."

Without hearing a word from her man, she hung up. He quietly and unemotionally closed his phone, choosing to remain speechless.

Chapter 68

"CONCRETE PLANS ESTABLISHED FOR A MEETING"

Colerain was sitting at his island, serenely working on the *New York Times* Sunday crossword puzzle. This huge Sunday challenge was virtually impossible for him to complete. If he would be able to fill in two-thirds of the blocks, he could claim partial success. Just as he was filling in 52 down, nine letters, the capital city of Mongolia with Ulan Bator, his cell phone began to vibrate with its rumbling sound. It seemed ready to begin a walk across the island. Before he could answer the device, it began to play the selected ring tone, "breaking beats." He read the caller ID screen and it displayed the words "no data," therefore, he chose not to answer. Within seconds he heard the ping-ding sound indicating that he had been left an instant message. Going into the phone's menu, he clicked Messages, then Text Messages, and finally he opened the inbox and read the most recent message. It read: Mr. Pike, answer. L.T.

Taking a deep breath, he pushed the call-back feature.

L.T. immediately answered. "Mr. Pike, it's okay. I am not calling to threaten you or to compromise your freedom. I want to have dinner with you, tomorrow, 7:00 p.m., at the Eastern Winds Asian restaurant. The restaurant is located on Bessemer Avenue, about two blocks east of your Zapatas." The woman spoke in a relaxed and dignified-sounding voice, somehow alarming Colerain.

He inquired, "Will you please reveal who you are?"

She casually responded, "I did not want to use my personal or business phone to call you. I did not want to be identified with the caller ID feature. I could have used Tiumes' phone, but that is all traceable. So I purchased a 90-minute-filled phone at the local Wal-Mart. No features, no ID. Let me tell you something, in line, right in front of me, an Al-Qaida-looking man bought seventeen of the same types of phone that I was buying. Aren't some of those people terrorists? And can't they detonate car bombs by using cell phones as the triggers? I don't know what is wrong with the security in this country. The cashier just rang up the sale and never asked him a question. What a shame," she rambled.

"Oh, Mr. Pike, my dear Mr. Pike, you will gain all of the information that you desire tomorrow, at our dinner," she added, sweetly.

Before he could respond, the phone call abruptly ended. Sitting with both hands holding his now pounding head, he was at a loss for words. This woman, I have never heard her voice before. It sounded as though English may have not been her primary language. A few of her words may have displayed an Asian accent of some kind. Then again, maybe not Asian, but Russian or Eastern European, he mused.

"Oh shit!" he said out loud to himself.

Chapter 69

"AN EVENING LACED WITH INTRIGUE AT EASTERN WINDS"

The weather for this Monday evening in early September seemed perfect as he walked along Bessemer Avenue. He deftly folded the cuffs of his long-sleeved, light blue dress shirt, up one turn, revealing his tanned and powerful wrists. His taupe-colored slacks and heather brown leather belt coordinated seamlessly. Medium brown clogs and brown socks completed his ensemble. He looked good.

As he entered the Eastern Winds restaurant, he requested from the hostess a table for two near the garishly decorated rear wall. He selected his seat to allow his back to be toward the wall, offering him an expansive view of the restaurant's entryway and main dining area. While glancing at the endless dinner offerings and modest prices of the menu, he poured himself a cup of steaming hot green tea. Beef and broccoli on steamed rice and maybe a vegetable egg roll sounded appetizing, he thought.

He had no idea as to the identity of his dinner mate. He was able to stop his normal scanning of the dining facility and concentrated upon the menu and his approaching rendezvous. The woman knows him, therefore she would need to locate and approach him. Very simple process, he thought. While he glanced again at his menu, a quiet voice startled him.

"Hello, Mr. Pike. I am L.T.—Leng Tyans. May I join you," she asked.

Recovering slightly, he spoke. "Of course, Ms. Tyans, please be seated," as he rose and gently pulled out her chair to assist her in seating. Always be the gentleman, he maintained to himself.

While she settled into her seat, he offered, "Green tea?"

"Yes, thank you," came her demure reply.

(H.M. [her mom])

"Please call me Leng, Colerain. I believe that we are quickly going to learn a great deal about each other. We will become closer, close as two beautiful koi in a splendid summer pond," she cooed.

"Leng," he began, "you seem to know so much about me already. You are in possession of a rather extensive range of power in reference to my tenuous personal freedom."

"Dear man, please do not be annoyed about that remote possibility at this time. Why can't we just enjoy a wonderful dining experience and some stimulating conversation? We will entertain those other matters when the timing is more appropriate," she suggested.

Their dinner entrees were selected, served, and enjoyed. The delicious green tea provided was the only beverage necessary to make the dining experience completely satisfying. Leng complimented him for his skill and dexterity in easily handling his chopsticks. Better than most Westerners, she stated. They also generously shared and sampled each other's dinner selections. Colerain did order the beef dish, and Leng chose sweet and sour chicken with copious amounts of steamed white rice that was shared.

Their conversational topics ranged from North American artists, including Grant Wood, Winslow Homer, and Andrew Wyeth, to the one-week-old National Football League season. He found the conversation to be quite stimulating and encouraging. He actually enjoyed the dinner chit-chat.

Colerain surmised that Leng Tyans appeared to be around fifty years of age. Her dark brown hair was stylishly cut short. Age appropriate, he thought. Her comely face did assist in revealing her probable age, and besides, he thought that she wore more than a modest amount of make-up. Precisely manicured French-tipped nails topped her relatively smallish hands, which were covered with an assemblage of golden-colored rings. Whoa, way too much jewelry, was his initial unstated opinion.

Her black business suit was well tailored and obviously quite expensive. A light pink blouse opened to her breast line revealing what he thought were surgically enhanced breasts. Somewhat overdone, he thought, but still an attractive woman.

Peering across the cleared table, she spoke softly and directly to him. "Mr. Pike, I was there when you ended the life of my daughter. I can describe every detail of your actions. The strangling, the removal and folding of her clothing, the posing of her body, the drawing, everything. Once, I thought that you definitely heard my movements, but her cat Nitro, caught your attention instead with his prancing around in her house."

Barely able to speak, he whispered, "You are Tiumes Maggic's mother, oh my God."

Leng unexpectedly stood and without warning, began to address the other patrons in the restaurant. In a clear and resonating voice she said, "Excuse me, ladies and gentlemen, I'd like to make an announcement. The gentleman that I am dining with is Mr. Colerain Pike. At this moment, I am professing my undying love for him."

Stunned briefly, many in the restaurant then began a rousing round of applause for the speaker that lasted for at least thirty seconds.

"Why did you say that?'" he implored.

"Darling, I made that public display of affection so that many potential witnesses could identify you if anything unpleasant ever happened to me. You would easily be implicated. Not that you would do me any harm, but I have always learned to protect myself," she explained.

"You amaze me, Leng," was his direct reply.

"Mr. Pike, thank you. I would like to tell you about my daughter. Yesterday, I had her body cremated. As a Buddhist, even though she had no fervor for our religion, that is our custom. I had some monks from my temple enhance the ceremony with comforting chants. Her good energies had to be released, if she really had any," she recounted.

After a slight pause, she continued. "What you could never have realized is that I passionately hated that little bitch. She was a selfish, nasty tart who derived insatiable pleasure from mocking, using, and occasionally physically abusing me, her mother. These behaviors began when she was in junior high school, while I slavishly worked to provide her with everything and anything that she demanded or required. I tried so hard to be a good mother. I ended up being her personal servant. She appreciated nothing and demanded more. She never allowed me to be anything more than some unassimilated immigrant. I'm happy that she is dead. The slutty, man-collecting and abusing bitch deserved to die." Then Leng became profoundly quiet and reserved.

Colerain stared at the woman, unable to produce a single syllable.

She smiled brightly at him and commented, "Don't worry, sir, I will never expose you. You have to understand my love, that I have wanted you and loved you from the beginning of the period of time that you showed interest in my daughter. She told me of your intelligence, your talents, your generosity, and your skills at lovemaking. Those things I wanted and needed, yet you provided them to my unappreciative offspring. Besides," she continued, "I must have you, for you are now IN MY HEAD."

The end

Lightning Source UK Ltd.
Milton Keynes UK
UKHW040614281119
354396UK00002B/320/P

9 781643 765570